Panic in the
WILD WATERS

Lee Roddy

PUBLISHING

Colorado Springs, Colorado

Panic in the Wild Waters
Copyright ©1995 by Lee Roddy
All rights reserved. International copyright secured.

Library of Congress Cataloging-in Publication Data

Roddy, Lee, 1921–
    Panic in the wild waters / Lee Roddy.
        p. cm.—(A Ladd family adventure ; 12)
    Summary: The Ladd family's Hawaii adventures are ending, but not
before they once more swim with the whales, scuba dive, and outwit their
antagonists—two drug-smuggling sea-turtle poachers.
    ISBN 1-56179-392-2
    [1. Hawaii—Fiction. 2. Mystery and detective stories.] I. Title. II. Series:
Roddy, Lee, 1921– Ladd family adventure.
PZ7.R6Pan   1995
[Fic]—dc20   95-10951
                                                                          CIP
                                                                          AC

Published by Focus on the Family Publishing,
Colorado Springs, Colorado 80995.
Distributed in the U.S.A. and Canada by Word Books, Dallas, Texas.

The author is represented by the literary agency of Alive Communications,
P.O. Box 49068, Colorado Springs, CO 80920.

This is a work of fiction, and any resemblance between the characters in this book
and real persons is coincidental.

Editor: Ron Klug
Cover Illustration: Paul Casale
Cover Design: James Lebbad

Printed in the United States of America

95 96 97 98 99/10 9 8 7 6 5 4 3 2 1

To Patrick Roddy,
my firstborn grandson,
for bringing such great joy
to all of us

CONTENTS

Chapter One

DANGER BELOW!

Trailing bubbles from his scuba* gear, Josh Ladd swam out of the underwater cave side by side with his best friend, Tank Catlett. They were just in time to see three green sea turtles gliding by in Hawaii's clear blue waters. One turtle was missing a flipper, which may have been bitten off by a shark.

Glancing to his right, Josh saw his older sister, Tiffany, and her new Alaskan girlfriend, Alicia Wharton, in their scuba gear. They were floating underwater, their backs to the open sea as they examined something on the black volcanic reef before them.

That's when Josh saw the shark.

It appeared from nowhere—a long, slender phantom that glided slowly and silently toward the backs of the unsuspecting girls twenty feet away.

Josh's muffled shout and abrupt actions caught his

---

*The definition and pronunciation of words marked by asterisks are contained in a glossary at the end of the book.

diving buddy's attention. Tank kicked his legs hard, his flippers driving him close to where he faced Josh.

Josh answered Tank's unspoken question by thrusting his right arm straight out from the shoulder with his fist closed. It was the underwater signal for *Danger!*

As Tank whirled about to see for himself, Josh hurriedly snatched his knife from where it was strapped to his right leg above the ankle. The blade, usually used to free a diver from underwater hazards, could also be a signaling device. Josh used it to tap sharply on the metal air cylinder strapped to his back.

Both girls turned at the sound. Josh repeated his danger signal, swinging his arm to point at the shark. He saw the girls' startled reaction and began swimming toward them, the knife in his hand. It was no real defense against a shark, but it was all Josh had.

Out of his wraparound mask, Josh saw that Tank was swimming fast to keep up with him. Josh focused his attention on the shark. He noticed with relief that it didn't have the distinctive stripes that marked it as a tiger, a known man-eater. He knew it wasn't the dreaded great white, because they are rare in Hawaii.

Josh decided it was a gray reef shark, an aggressive but usually harmless type. Still, the way this six-foot specimen headed for the girls gave Josh the impression that it might attack.

Josh's blue eyes shifted to the girls. His sister faced the approaching shark and started slowly moving her fins, propelling herself toward the surface, her back to the reef. The shark swam straight toward Alicia Wharton.

She started to back into a shallow crevice, but that was impossible with her fins on. She rolled over from a standing position and swam into the hole. She whirled around, her legs drawn up tight against her chest, and literally shoved the shark's nose with her feet.

With a flip of its tail, the shark whirled away, giving Josh and Tank time to reach the girl. Tank drew his own knife and turned to face the shark, which had started to circle back. Josh motioned for Alicia to come out of the hole. As she hesitated, he swung his right arm in front of his body, thumb up, meaning she was to start upward.

Slowly, she obeyed, gray eyes wide through her mask. Josh turned to join Tank in facing the shark. Their backs were to the lava reef, with the girl between them. In an upright position, they began moving their fins, easing toward their boat waiting on the surface.

Josh seldom got angry, but he was seething because he was sure what had attracted the shark to Alicia while it ignored Tiffany's escape. Josh usually got along with everyone, but from the moment the reckless tomboy, Alicia, had arrived from Alaska yesterday with her father, she had rubbed Josh the wrong way.

I knew she was trouble from the moment we met, Josh reminded himself, still watching the shark. *She's so stubborn! She insisted on using that old regulator with a faulty O-ring, even after I warned her it could attract sharks. But she wouldn't listen. I just pray that we get out of this alive, and she goes back to Alaska real soon.*

It seemed to take forever for the brightness of the sun on the surface to show that the trip to the top was nearly over. Josh was fearful that the shark would attack before they reached the safety of their boat, because the creature stayed close. Its large, dark, expressionless eyes were obviously focused on Alicia in preference to the boys.

At last Alicia's head broke the surface. The boys kept their faces underwater to make sure there was no last-minute attack. When Alicia's fins left the water, the shark turned and swam away.

Josh and Tank broke the surface together. They ripped off their regulators and let out joyous shouts of relief. Their part-Hawaiian guide, Kapali*, used his great upper body strength to pull the boys into the boat with him and the girls. Kapali had been hired by Alicia's father to drive a car or boat, as his daughter required.

Josh tried to control his annoyance with Alicia, but Tank verbally lashed out at her. "You crazy wahine*!" he cried. "That shark was after you because of that old regulator you insisted on using! Josh warned you earlier that there's a piston in the first stage of the regulator. It's controlled by springs and O-rings. Low-frequency vibration is what attracts sharks. They think it's an injured fish, and . . ."

"Don't yell at me!" Alicia broke in, her face still pale in the warm sun. "That was a harmless shark!"

"How do you know that?" Tank demanded before Josh could say anything.

"I've studied sharks!" Alicia replied hotly. Her short blond hair was plastered over her forehead. "That wasn't a man-eater!"

Josh commented, "It still could have taken a bite out of us!"

Tiffany's long, slender body was encased in a pink wet suit. She cautioned, "Hey, you guys! Take it easy on her!"

Josh forced himself to say calmly, "It was an unnecessary risk. Alicia, your father is rich enough to have rented you a new regulator so you wouldn't have to use that old one."

"I've had this for years, and I like it!" Alicia snapped, thrusting her face belligerently toward the dark-haired boy. "That's why I brought it from Alaska!"

"It almost got you chewed up!" Tank cried, his voice fast and his tone sharp. That was in contrast to his usual slow, easygoing manner of speaking.

Kapali commented, "You haoles* are all alive, yeah?"

Josh looked at Kapali and realized that the Hawaiian way of accepting things philosophically was the right thing to do in this case. "You're right. That's all that really matters," Josh said. "Let's head for home."

Tempers had cooled somewhat by the time the boat was docked. Carrying their diving gear, the friends headed for the rental car, a Jeep, parked near a sugarcane* field. However, as Alicia and Kapali moved ahead, Tiffany dropped back to walk with her brother and Tank.

"You guys were pretty hard on her," Tiffany rebuked them. "She's been my pen pal for a couple of years, and I invited her to visit us . . ."

"She's trouble," Josh interrupted.

"You said it!" Tank added, rubbing his sunburned nose. It was always peeling from the Hawaiian sun, just as his blond hair had been bleached nearly white. "When is she going back to Alaska?"

"In a week," Tiffany said, shaking her short brunette hair, which was drying fast.

"She'll bury us in trouble during that time," Tank grumbled. "You wait and see."

"Don't be like that," Tiffany said sharply. "Anyway, Dad said you boys were to treat her like any guest."

Josh slowly nodded. "Okay," he said with a sigh. "I'll get along with her—if she'll let me."

Tank snorted to show his disgust. "She'll never do that, and you can bet on it. Her rich daddy has spoiled her. I bet nobody can get along with her."

"I can," Tiffany replied. "I like her even though she's a little rough around the edges. So please try."

Tank shrugged. "I guess I can do it for a week, but I want to stay as far away from her as possible."

"Thanks," Tiffany said and rejoined her friend, giving Josh an opportunity to study the visitor walking ahead of him.

Alicia was only twelve, but she was as tall, though not as slender, as Tiffany, who was fourteen. Motherless, Alicia often flew with her father to the various lodges he owned in Alaska's vast wilderness areas. Earlier she had bragged that she could fly her bush pilot father's float plane. She claimed that he let her take the controls even though she was too young to solo.

Alicia was too independent and pushy to suit Josh. He and Tank loved adventure, as Alicia obviously did. Yet, she had a reckless streak that concerned Josh.

He and Tank had been close friends most of their lives. When they were babies, they often shared the same playpen. Growing up, they had become inseparable, being in the same classrooms and enjoying the Southern California beaches together. They had never been separated except for the few months after Tank's father was transferred to Hawaii to manage a department store. Those had been the most miserable days of the boys' lives. Then Mr. Ladd had bought a tourist publication in Waikiki*, and the Ladd family had rejoined the Catletts in Honolulu*.

Together again, Josh and Tank walked in warm friendship under Hawaii's glorious clear skies, truly enjoying being alive.

Tank intruded on Josh's thoughts. "Someday I'd like to see Alaska, wouldn't you?"

Josh's eyes lit up. "Sure! What great adventures we could have together!"

"Alaska's our biggest state, you know, far bigger than Texas. And most of it's real primitive, like the West used to be a hundred or so years ago."

Josh nodded. "I hear it's so big that there are lots of places with no roads, so you have to go by plane or boat."

"Boy!" Tank exclaimed. "Wouldn't that be the greatest place you can imagine to explore together?"

"The greatest!"

The boys had fallen somewhat behind the girls and the driver, who were walking through a sugarcane field toward the car. Josh stopped abruptly, cocking his head.

"What do you hear?" Tank asked as Josh turned to face the sea.

"Sounds like a boat," Josh replied.

Tank shaded his eyes and studied the water. "I don't see it."

"It just started up, over there by that cove. See it now? Two men are putting out to sea."

The boys stopped to watch as a twelve-foot-long motorboat headed toward the mouth of the cove. A local* sat in the bow. A haole steered from the stern.

Josh observed, "I guess they're fishermen."

"Probably—but suppose they aren't?" Tank asked.

Grinning at his friend, Josh said, "You mean your imagination is working overtime, and you want to go see what they were doing."

Tank studied the boat. It was almost out of sight, hugging the shoreline instead of heading into open water. "Wouldn't hurt to check, would it?"

"I guess not." Josh raised his voice so the others could hear him. "Tank and I are going to see where that little boat came from. We'll meet you at the car."

Alicia replied, "Don't be long!"

Tank lowered his voice and mimicked the girl, "*Don't be long*! Who does she think she is, anyway?"

Josh tried to be fair, pushing aside his earlier feelings. "She's an only child with no mother and a rich father who gives her everything she wants. She probably doesn't know any better."

"I just wish we didn't have to spend the week with her," Tank muttered, "but this morning my dad also said we should be nice to her and show her everything she wants to see. Naturally, she wants to see Hawaii underwater, with all its dangers. We got off lucky with that shark."

Leaving their gear in a pile on the ground, Tank and Josh pushed their way through the last of the sugarcane. Soon they stood on a small rise overlooking the cove. "I wonder what our dads talked to Mr. Wharton about when they all went out to dinner last night," Josh said.

"I don't know. Dad usually takes Mom with him when we've got visitors."

"Same with my mom. Hey, look down there!" Josh pointed to a small gully leading to the cove. "I think it's what's left of a sea turtle. Let's take a look."

"It's illegal to kill them," Tank said as the boys hurried down the gully toward the cove.

"Hawaii's sea turtles are officially considered threatened but not yet endangered," Josh agreed. "Those men we saw in the boat must have killed this one."

"Butchered it, too," Tank observed as they drew close. "That's the shell turned upside down. Those men just took the meat. So that must mean they're not professional poachers who would sell the shell for ornamental things."

"Whether they're professional poachers or not, this poor turtle's life is over."

The boys stood in silence, contemplating the remains of a harmless sea creature. Both boys had seen nature programs on television about turtles. The films showed tiny baby sea turtles emerging from their sandy cradle on shore to immediately face a dangerous world. The newly hatched turtles instantly began a desperate, instinctive race to the water while birds and ground predators swooped down on them.

The remains of the two-foot-long specimen at the boys' feet showed that this turtle had escaped those early dangers, plus sharks and other perils of the sea, only to die at the hands of human adversaries.

"Makes me angry," Josh said grimly. "Killing a poor defenseless creature like this."

"Me, too. Boy, would I like to find out who did this and see them in jail!"

With a sigh, Josh nodded. "But I guess we'd better report this to the authorities. Let them handle it."

The boys turned around, then stopped in alarm.

"Listen!" Josh exclaimed. "It's the boat! Those men are coming back. Let's get out of here!"

The boys started to run just as the boat rounded the

corner and reentered the cove. The haole suddenly pointed to the running boys and changed the boat's direction sharply, heading straight toward shore.

"They've seen us!" Tank cried, looking for the Jeep, where Kapali and the girls were waiting. It was out of sight beyond the tall sugarcane plants. "They're coming after us!"

Josh nodded and kept running. He shot a glance over his shoulder. Sunlight reflected off a big knife in the hands of the haole, who leaped from the boat onto the shore. Josh remembered what had happened to the turtle.

The second man jumped from the boat, making Josh suddenly aware of another danger.

He called a warning. "Tank, we're in trouble! They're trying to cut us off from our car!"

Chapter Two

FLYING INTO TROUBLE

Tank started to pant from running so fast. "We can't let them do that!"

"We can't stop them, so we'll have to go around."

"What about our diving gear?"

"Don't worry about that. After we get to the car, we'll circle back for our equipment. Just don't let them cut us off or catch us!"

Josh's eyes probed for another avenue of escape. This was totally unfamiliar territory, without a house or person in sight. Kapali and the girls were too far away to hear even if the boys called to them. Josh and Tank were on their own with their pursuers closing fast.

The men had cut off the boys' escape on the right. Straight ahead, a row of ironwood trees* offered temporary shelter. But what was behind them? Josh couldn't see. Going that way could lead them into a trap.

The ocean lay behind the boys, but they couldn't outswim a motorboat. To the left and inland from where they had been walking, the ground rose slightly toward a series of tumbled boulders stretched across the land.

"That way!" Josh yelled, turning to the left. He dashed toward the boulders, hearing Tank panting behind.

One of their pursuers let out an angry roar, followed by coarse language and violent threats.

Josh neared the boulders, which had been smoothed by past high tides. Smaller rocks around the boulders warned Josh that he would have to watch his step. He risked a glance back. "They're still coming," he told Tank.

"Keep running," Tank shouted, "and do it faster so I don't have to step on you when I pass."

Josh almost smiled at his friend's attempt at humor when Tank was obviously frightened. "Watch your step!" Josh warned as he began picking his way over the smaller rocks. Even as he spoke, he stubbed his right toe on a stone imbedded in the sand.

Tank yelled, "Watch out!"

The warning was useless. Josh had already started to fall forward. He broke his fall with his hands, which were instantly scoured by the coarse sand. He leaped up, picking up the rock that had tripped him.

"Quick!" Josh urged, prying other stones loose with the toe of his tennis shoes. "Grab a handful of rocks and duck between those two big boulders. Maybe we can drive them off!"

Hurriedly gathering as many stones as they could carry, the boys slid between two boulders about four feet high.

"Aim at their feet and legs," Josh instructed. "Don't try to hurt them. Just make them back off. Ready?"

When Tank nodded, Josh stood up with a rock in each hand. Only his head and the upper part of his chest showed.

"Now!" he cried, throwing toward the stocky haole, who was a few steps in front of the slender local.

Josh's first rock fell short, but the next one smashed into the haole's shin. He yelped in pain, dropped his knife, and hopped about on one leg, swearing terribly.

His companion, trailing a few steps behind, dodged as Tank's first missile whizzed by his knee.

"Keep throwing!" Josh urged, putting action to his words. He threw two more times, making the men retreat. When they were out of throwing distance, the men turned around and yelled threats.

"Don't either of yah ever come back!" the stocky one roared. "We know what yah look like, but ain't nobody goin' to be able to recognize neither of yah if'n we ever git our hands on yah!"

"You heard him!" the slender man shouted. He picked up his companion's fallen knife and handed it to him as he hobbled away, favoring his injured leg.

The boys didn't reply. Breathing hard, they stood ready behind their barricade until the men had reached their boat. Then they laughed with relief and clapped each other on their backs.

"Wow!" Tank exclaimed. "That was pretty exciting!"

Josh inspected his palms where he had fallen. They were red and a little sore where the skin had been broken. "Yes, but you know what?"

"What?"

"Those poachers belong in jail, both for killing that turtle and for chasing us with that big knife."

Now that the danger was over, Tank said teasingly, "Great idea! I've heard of a citizen's arrest, so maybe you could just walk up to them and ... "

"Oh, all right!" Josh interrupted, giving his friend a playful punch on the shoulder. "But I sure would like to see them arrested. The least we can do is report this to the police or somebody when we call them about finding that turtle."

The boys retrieved their diving gear where they had dropped it, occasionally looking back to make sure the poachers hadn't followed them. There was no sign of pursuit when they came to what Kapali had earlier laughingly referred to as "a road." It was barely two tracks where off-road vehicles had ventured.

The boys stopped to rest by a small bridge where the trade winds whistled through the needles on ironwood trees. A sign that Josh remembered from the walk in, still proclaimed *Road Narrows*. Someone had hand-lettered *Road Awful* across it.

The boys were tired from carrying their scuba gear by the time they reached the Jeep at the edge of the sugarcane field.

"What kept you two?" Tiffany demanded in the bossy, big-sister tone she sometimes used with Josh.

"We got chased by two men who had killed a sea turtle," Tank began.

Josh joined in, telling what had happened. Kapali loaded the boys' diving gear into the Jeep with the other equipment.

When they had finished their report, Alicia said, "Wish I had been with you. I would really have hit them with rocks."

Tank snapped, "I suppose you could have done better than we did?"

"Bet I could! You want to have a rock-throwing contest?" she challenged. "I can do anything you two can—and do it better."

Josh saw Tank roll his eyes heavenward as though he couldn't believe this tomboy from Alaska. And she was going to be around for another week!

Tiffany ended the verbal clashes as she climbed into the Jeep. "This isn't a contest, so let's settle down."

The others entered the vehicle, and soon they were bouncing along a bumpy, rutted road that snaked through the twelve-foot-tall sugarcane.

As the Jeep neared the highway, Alicia announced, "We've got to come back here because of that shark."

"What?" Josh asked in disbelief.

Alicia nodded. "My father always says when a horse throws you, it's important to get right back on so you won't be afraid. Same thing applies to that shark that chased us out of the water."

"That shark is long gone by now," Josh replied.

"Besides," Tank added, "even if it isn't, we're not going to dive there with you again!"

"I'll get another regulator," Alicia assured him. "One without a faulty O-ring. The only thing you boys have to be concerned about is whether you're scared to dive where we saw the shark."

"Scared?" Tank sputtered. "We're not scared, are we?"

Josh answered carefully, "Not really, but we sure don't want to do anything foolish."

"Good!" Alicia said enthusiastically. "That's settled."

"Not quite," Tiffany commented. "You boys are forgetting about those poachers."

Josh reflected on that before answering. "I'm sure they won't bother us if we're all together, especially with Kapali along."

The driver looked into the rearview mirror and smiled. "Do I get to have a say in this? I mean, what happens if all four of you are diving and I'm sitting there all alone in the boat when those men come along?"

"They never saw you," Tank reminded Kapali. "You and the girls had already walked out of sight before those men came along, so they shouldn't bother you."

Kapali seemed satisfied. He looked at Alicia. "Your daddy hired me to take you wherever you want, so I guess if you want to come back here for another dive, I'm willing."

Tiffany said to Alicia, "I thought you wanted to visit some of the other islands and do some more undersea diving?"

"I do, but we've still got time to do all of those things before Daddy and I leave for Alaska."

Tank told Alicia, "We're flying back to Honolulu this afternoon, so when do you plan to come back here?"

"As soon as possible."

Tiffany said, "I don't think it's a good idea . . ."

Alicia broke in. "Where's your spirit of adventure, Tiffany?"

"I'm not like my brother or the rest of you," Tiffany explained. "I prefer to read or hear about other people's experiences."

Josh said, "Tank and I want to see those poachers caught, so we'd like to come back."

"Yeah!" Tank chimed in. "We'll come back with cops!"

Kapali commented, "I don't think the police handle poacher cases. I believe it's under the jurisdiction of DAR/DLNR. That stands for the Division of Aquatic Resources, Department of Land and Natural Resources. Anyway, Josh, you can ask the operator . . ."

"Look!" Josh broke in, pointing. "See that car turning left up there? That looks like the same two men who chased us. See them, Tank?"

"I didn't get a good look, but the driver is a haole and the other guy is a local. Kapali, let's get a closer look at them."

"Now, just a minute, Tank!" Alicia said brusquely. "You're not paying for this Jeep or the driver!"

Josh said mildly, "You're right, but I think that Tank just meant that you might like to know what those men look like—you know, in case you run into them when we come back to make that dive."

"Yeah," Tank agreed with a grin. "That's what I meant."

"Well," Alicia said, "why didn't you say so, Tank?" Without waiting for an answer, she told Kapali to follow the other car. It was a dusty old sedan with fenders rusted through from the salt air.

Josh leaned forward, excitement rising as he peered through the Jeep's dirty windshield. The other vehicle was some distance ahead, but the side road had little traffic, so the Jeep rapidly closed the distance.

"I'm pretty sure it's the same two men," Josh said a minute later as Kapali slowed behind the other car.

"The driver is looking at us in the rearview mirror," Tank commented. "I think he's wondering why we came up on him so fast but aren't passing."

"If he'd just turn around . . . ," Josh said, then left his thought unfinished as the driver glanced over his shoulder. "Yes! That's the same man! The one with the knife, the one I hit in the leg with a rock."

"Slow up, Kapali!" Alicia ordered. "Don't make him suspicious."

Tiffany added, "He might still have that knife."

As the Jeep slowed and the other man looked back,

Tank exclaimed, "That's the other guy, for sure! Josh, I wonder if they recognized us."

"I don't know," Josh admitted.

Tiffany suggested with a touch of fear in her voice, "Let's get out of here—fast!"

Alicia nodded and motioned to the driver, who braked hard and made a fast U-turn.

Josh joined the others in looking back, wondering if the poachers would follow them. An uneasy feeling gripped him until he realized that the other vehicle was still going in the other direction. As the Jeep rapidly returned to the main road, Josh kept glancing over his shoulder, but the poachers did not follow. He decided that the men must live somewhere in the area.

Kapali stopped the Jeep at the first public phone, and Josh told the operator about the turtle. She connected him with the Hawaii Division of Land and Natural Resources, a Division of Forestry and Wildlife for the Kauai* District.

There Josh spoke with a man who identified himself as Gary Browning, an aquatic biologist. He listened to Josh's report.

"I'm glad you called," Mr. Browning said when Josh had finished. "That's the third turtle reported slaughtered this month. Apparently, the poachers aren't commercial, because they're taking only the meat even though there's a market overseas for the shells. They must be locals."

"One looked like he was a local," Josh agreed. "The

other was a haole. Didn't sound as though he was very well educated."

"Your description will be helpful," Mr. Browning replied. "I'll notify our enforcement division because they have investigative and arrest powers. I'd like to set up an appointment for you to meet with them and me. Right now you can tell me how to find the place where they killed that turtle. I may need to perform an autopsy on it."

"That place is pretty hard to find, but I'll try," Josh replied and gave directions as best he could.

When he finished, Mr. Browning thanked Josh and added, "Our enforcement officer will want to ask you boys questions. Where can I reach you?"

Josh gave his Honolulu phone number, and Mr. Browning said he would call Josh there. They hung up. Back in the Jeep, Josh repeated the conversation he'd had with the biologist. "I just hope they catch those poachers," he finished as the Jeep headed toward the airport.

Usually, Josh realized, when a bunch of kids his age got together, there was a lot of laughing, talking, and singing. But this was different.

The two girls talked quietly, ignoring the boys. Josh could still sense the tension with Alicia. He didn't think there was much chance that the shark would return on their next dive because there wouldn't be any harmonics from a faulty O-ring to attract it.

He was much more interested in having the turtle poachers caught. The idea of someone killing the harmless sea creatures concerned Josh.

Alicia also bothered him. He didn't want any trouble with her, but she seemed to bring it with her wherever she went. Josh sighed. *Another whole week!*

As the plane lifted off from the Lihue* Airport, Josh had no idea that he and Tank were heading toward a huge surprise—and much more trouble than Alicia would ever be.

Chapter Three

TERRIBLE NEWS

Josh had the first inkling that something was wrong when everyone arrived back at the three-story apartment building where the Ladds and Catletts lived at the foot of Diamond Head*.

As Josh and the others climbed out of the rental car that Kapali had picked up at the Honolulu Airport, Tank's older sister, Marsha, was waiting for them. She was shorter than Tiffany but about the same age. With only a brief greeting to the others, Marsha turned to her brother.

"Tank, something's going on with Mom and Dad. He phoned a while ago and talked to Mom. She was all upset."

"Upset? What about?" Tank asked.

"Mom wouldn't tell me a thing. She said it would have to wait until you and Dad got home tonight."

"Maybe somebody is coming to visit," Tank guessed.

"Mom likes visitors, so I think this was something she didn't expect or like."

Tank tried again. "Maybe one of our relatives on the

23

Mainland is sick."

"I think Mom would have told me that," Marsha answered. "But whatever it is, she tried to put on a brave face when I pushed her to tell, only she wouldn't. Maybe she'll tell you."

"Yeah. I'll try. Josh, I'll be back as soon as possible." He and Marsha hurried off together.

"What's that all about?" Tiffany asked as she and Alicia, who was spending the night, climbed the outside concrete stairs to their second-story apartment.

Josh, trailing behind the girls, said, "I'll give Tank a few minutes, then I'll call him and see what he's found out."

The girls and Josh removed their shoes and left them outside the door in the Oriental fashion practiced by many people in Hawaii.

Josh opened the door and called, "Mom, we're home."

There was no answer, but a note on the refrigerator disclosed that she had gone to the library and would be back in time to start dinner.

As the girls crossed the living room and headed down the hallway to Tiffany's bedroom, the telephone rang.

"I'll get it," Josh said. "It's probably Tank."

It wasn't. Josh heard the person on the other end of the line say, "This is Gary Browning, the aquatic biologist with the DAR/DLNR. We talked earlier today."

"Yes, I remember. Did you catch those poachers?"

"Not yet. I tried to find the place where you said you had found that turtle carcass, but I couldn't."

"As I told you before, it's pretty hard to locate. I'll try to give you better directions."

"Thanks, but I'd rather meet with you and your friend. What was his name?"

"Tank Catlett."

"Tank. Anyway, do you two plan to fly back from Oahu* to Kauai anytime soon?"

"Yes. Some of us are going back to the same place, probably tomorrow."

"I wouldn't go there alone if I were you. Those poachers threatened you. Maybe they'll act on that."

"Oh, we're not going back to the turtle place, exactly. We're going nearby, to where we were diving."

"Good! When you know your time of arrival on Kauai, give me a call, and I'll meet you with an enforcement officer from our office. We can all go down to the site together."

Josh agreed, hung up, and dialed the Catletts' apartment. The radio in Tiffany's room started blaring loud music. He ignored it, hearing the phone ringing in his ear and also downstairs. The open louvered windows in the Catletts' apartment allowed the sound to carry through the Ladds' lanai* screen door.

When the phone had rung six times, Josh scowled. *That's funny. Why don't they answer?*

He hung up, fighting an uneasy feeling. Sliding open the screen door, he sat down on the lanai*. It was located directly over the Catletts' lanai on the ground floor. Josh could hear voices from Tank's apartment, but he couldn't make out the words. Josh looked up at Diamond Head's massive bulk towering above him.

Wonder what's keeping Tank? Josh asked himself, leaning forward to look down at the empty lanai below.

Josh lifted his gaze as two other friends started up the cul-de-sac*, carrying skateboards. They walked between the first apartment building on their right and a high fence of bamboo and oleanders* on the left.

Roger Okamoto and Manuel Souza walked warily, as did most neighborhood boys who had to pass along a dense growth of oleanders, be-still trees*, and fifteen-foot-tall bamboo stalks. The foliage hid a fence and formed the boundary between the street and the unpopulated area at the base of Diamond Head.

Instinctively, Josh scanned the boundary and was relieved that there was no sign of King Kong, the neighborhood bully. Although only fourteen, Kong was six feet tall and weighed more than 200 pounds. He was known to pop out of the shrubbery and attack without warning. Usually, he did that only when a boy was alone.

"Hey, Josh! Get your board and come down," Roger called. He wore faded blue cutoffs and sandals but no shirt.

"I'm waiting for Tank," Josh called back.

"Wait down here with us," Roger urged. He was a third-generation Japanese-American and a Buddhist*. He lived on the third floor of the apartment building, above Josh and Tank.

When Josh hesitated, thinking about Tank's long delay, Manuel also called for Josh to come down.

"Okay, I'm coming," Josh replied. He stepped into his sandals outside the apartment door. They made slip-slapping sounds as Josh approached Roger and Manuel.

Manuel, of Portuguese descent, rested his bare feet on his board. He wore long print shorts without a shirt. He lived with his mother in a small board-and-batten* house down the street, near the opposite end of the cul-de-sac.

He asked, "How are you getting along with your sister's friend from Alaska?"

"Don't ask," Josh replied.

"That bad, huh?" Manuel asked with an understanding grin. He was considered smart, the most akamai* kid in school.

Josh didn't answer. Through the screen on the Catletts' open outside window, he could see Tank, his sister, and his mother. Tank jumped up and ran to the telephone, his motions showing that he was upset. Josh waited, expecting to hear the phone ring in his apartment, but it did not.

"Something's wrong in there," Manuel observed softly. "Do you know what it is?"

Josh shook his head and walked away so it wouldn't seem that he and the other two boys were eavesdropping. Josh quickly explained what Marsha had said before she and Tank had gone inside their apartment.

Mrs. Souza's voice drifted up the slight incline from her home to where the boys stood. "Manuel!" She dragged out the name, then added, "Time to come in."

Manuel started to leave, carrying his skateboard, just as Tiffany called from the lanai.

"Josh, Dad is on the phone. Wants to talk to you."

"Coming," he replied, heading for the stairs while Roger and Manuel walked down the cul-de-sac.

On the stairs, Josh met Alicia carrying his skateboard. He felt instant annoyance that she hadn't asked him to borrow it.

"I won't hurt it," she said.

He didn't reply, but ran up the stairs, fighting an increased concern about why Tank hadn't called or come outside. Josh picked up the phone. "Hi, Dad."

"Son," Mr. Ladd's voice said in the boy's ear, "I'm going to Maui* on business. Want to come along?"

Josh replied without thinking. "Sure!" Then he remembered Alicia's determination to "get back on the horse that threw her." Josh added, "Wait a minute. It depends on when you're going."

"Day after tomorrow."

"That'll be fine, Dad."

"Good. Your sister and Alicia are welcome, too."

Josh closed his eyes and bit his tongue to keep from saying what he was thinking. Instead, he asked, "How about Tank?"

"Yes, of course. That goes without saying. Oh, what did he think about his father's offer?"

Josh gripped the phone tighter. "What offer?"

"Whoops!" Mr. Ladd exclaimed. "I apparently spoke too soon. Sorry, son. Well, I'll be home in a little . . . "

"Wait, Dad! Don't hang up! What about Tank's father?"

"It wouldn't be right for me to say anything until Tank tells you. See you in a little while."

The phone went dead in Josh's hands. He stared at it as if willing it to tell what his father had left unsaid.

Now really concerned, Josh again dialed Tank's apartment. Again the phone rang repeatedly, but nobody answered it. *Something's very wrong,* he told himself. He hung up and returned to the lanai. The murmur of voices still drifted up from the apartment below. *I know they're there, so why aren't they answering?* he wondered.

He thought about going downstairs and knocking on Tank's door, but he sensed that that wouldn't be the right thing to do just now. So Josh let his gaze drift upward onto Diamond Head's towering hulk, then down to Alicia. She was just getting onto his skateboard in a manner that showed she was obviously experienced.

Letting his gaze move on, Josh saw Roger heading back up the cul-de-sac, skateboard under his arm. His eyes probed the be-still trees with their bright yellow flowers that fold up at night.

Suddenly, Kong stepped through a hole in the fence. Roger stopped as though he had seen a big bull emerge from the bamboo and oleanders. It was said that Kong's disposition was very even: always mad. He never lost a chance to terrorize a lone boy.

Only Kong's sister, mother, and teachers called him by his real first name of Kamuela*. Behind his back, he was called King Kong, after the monster gorilla of a 1930s movie.

"Hey, bruddah*," he growled to Roger. In his cutoff blue jeans with no shirt or shoes, Kong looked like a brown fireplug with huge feet. In fact, his feet were the biggest Josh had ever seen on any boy.

Roger warily nodded in acknowledgment of Kong's greeting, but said nothing.

Kong smiled without humor and spoke in Pidgin English*. "Why foh you got da kine* skateboard? Look like da one belong Kong. You steal, yeah?"

"This is my board," Roger replied, his voice a little shaky. "I made it myself."

"You call Kong da kine liar?"

"No, of course not ... "

Josh didn't hear any more. *Run, Roger!* he thought, anticipating what was going to happen.

Kong took a pair of black leather gloves from his back pocket. Slowly, he began pulling one over his hand, which was the size of a ripe coconut and just as hard.

Roger is not going to run, Josh realized. *But that means he doesn't have a chance against Kong by himself. If Tank were here, and we showed up together, Kong would back off. But . . . .* Josh stood up. *I'd better go try to help,* Josh told himself without enthusiasm. *Maybe Kong won't want to face two of us.*

Josh ran down the stairs without bothering to put on

his sandals. At the bottom, he stopped in surprise. Roger, outweighed by at least a hundred pounds, crouched before King Kong, hands up in a defensive stance that every boy in the neighborhood knew was useless against the bully.

But it was the sight of Alicia dropping Josh's skateboard and charging toward Kong that made Josh yell. "Alicia, stop! Stay back! You'll get hurt!"

She ignored him and wordlessly passed Roger to stand before Kong. Suddenly, her right hand shot out like a striking cobra, and she grabbed a handful of the bully's wild hair.

"Ouch!" he yelled as Alicia yanked so hard he had to bend his head to ease the pain. "Why foh you do dat, you pupule* wahine?"

"Why don't you pick on somebody your own size?" Alicia demanded, holding Kong at arm's length by his hair. "Like me, for instance," she added.

Josh arrived, panting a little from the sprint. He stopped beside Roger. "You okay?"

Roger nodded but didn't speak, and Josh saw great distress in his brown eyes.

"Go to your place," Josh suggested softly, giving Roger a gentle push on the shoulder. But Roger didn't move.

Kong yelled at Alicia, "Let go da kine hair!"

"I will when I'm ready," she replied. "Now, keep quiet so I won't have to hurt you."

Josh softly told her, "You'd better let him go."

"I should jerk him baldheaded," she said, giving

Kong's head a final shake before letting go. She raised her voice to Kong. "Get home before I lose my temper."

Josh held his breath as the big bully hesitated, great anger burning in his eyes. Then, without a word, he melted into the be-still trees, through the fence, and out of sight.

Roger, always shy around girls, asked Alicia with great emotion in his voice, "Why did you do that? Who asked you, huh?"

Alicia drew back, startled. "I just saved you ... "

"You have disgraced me!" Roger interrupted. "I didn't need your help!" He made a strangled sound and ran toward the apartment building.

"What's the matter with him?" Alicia asked Josh, brushing her hands.

"You humiliated him," Josh explained gently. "In his culture, that's about the worst thing you could do."

"What?" Alicia's tone suggested she couldn't believe Josh. "Would he rather have taken a beating?"

"I think he would have."

She opened her mouth as though to make an angry reply, then closed it so hard that her teeth snapped together. Wordlessly, she too ran toward the apartment building.

Josh stared after her, understanding that Alicia had meant well, but good intentions didn't always count. He sighed. *I just wish her time was up and she was heading back to Alaska. I wonder how much worse things can get while she's here.*

On the way back to his apartment, Josh looked at

Tank's door, concerned about what was going on behind it. The door burst open, and Tank rushed out. He glanced with wild eyes at Josh, but didn't seem to see him.

Tank turned and yelled over his shoulder. "No, Mom! No!" His voice was high and thin with pain and anger. "You and Dad did it once before! You can't do it again!"

Mrs. Catlett followed him outside. Her pretty face showed tear stains. "Tank, please try to understand! I'm not thrilled about it either, but . . . "

"No!" he interrupted, running toward Josh, who had stopped in shock and surprise.

"What's the matter?" Josh asked in alarm.

Tank cried wildly, "My dad's being transferred to Alaska, and I have to go, too!"

Chapter Four

A DESPERATE SITUATION

What?" Josh cried in disbelief.

"It's true! We're moving to Alaska!" Tank's voice shot up and his face contorted as though he was in pain. "Mom told Marsha and me a little about it. Then I called Dad to make sure."

Josh felt as though someone had kicked him in the stomach. "But why?"

"Dad told me that if a person wants to advance in the business, he doesn't dare turn down a promotion, no matter where it takes him. If Dad ever turned down any move, even to Alaska, he would never again be considered for any future promotion. He said that's how big corporations operate."

Josh stared at his friend, feeling so sick at heart that he was almost physically ill. Unpleasant memories washed over him like a mighty tide. He remembered how miserable he had felt during the only time in their lives when the boys were separated.

That was when Tank's family moved from California to Hawaii and before the Ladds had also unexpectedly moved there. The reunited boys had determined that they would never again be parted. But now that was changing, and there was nothing either boy could do about it.

That's the trouble with being a kid, Josh thought miserably. *Parents move, and kids have to go along, no matter how they feel.*

As the shock of Tank's terrible news struck him, Josh forgot Alicia. He wasn't aware that she was standing beside him until she spoke to Tank.

"It won't be as if you didn't know anybody in Alaska," she began cheerfully. "I'll be there. Maybe we can even go to the same school."

Tank snorted derisively and abruptly turned away. He took a few quick steps and smashed his fist into the nearest oleander.

Alicia asked innocently, "Why is he taking it so hard?"

"Because," Josh answered hotly, "it means he and I won't be together anymore! And we've been best friends since we were little kids. That's why!"

Alicia shrugged. "Tiffany told me you two are like David and Jonathan in the Bible. Even they got separated, just as everybody eventually does. But life goes on . . . "

Josh interrupted. "What do you know about it? Did you ever lose a best friend?"

She didn't answer for a long moment. Then she said softly, "Yes, when my mother died."

"Oh!" In his sudden shame, Josh barely spoke the word

aloud. He kicked himself mentally as Alicia turned and ran toward the apartment stairs.

Tank said miserably, "We've got to do something, Josh. We can't let it happen—not again."

Nodding, Josh walked to his friend and laid a hand on his shoulder. "I'm willing. You know that. But . . . "

"No buts about it!" Tank broke in, his eyes showing sudden determination. "We've got to stop it!"

Josh took a slow, deep breath, trying to be logical and yet not further upset Tank. "I hate the idea of you moving away, but if your father has to take the job or lose a future with the company . . . "

"It doesn't matter!" Tank's voice took on a hard, firm edge. "I'm not going to let us be separated. Now, are you going to help think of a way or not?"

Josh flinched at Tank's sudden challenging tone, but Josh understood the pain and anger that caused it, so he nodded. "You know that I'm with you all the way."

For a long moment their eyes met, and Josh glimpsed a hint of Tank's unshed tears before he looked away. Josh felt a rush of hot moisture over his eyes that threatened to obscure his vision.

He suggested, "Let's go think this through."

"Yeah!" Tank replied, his voice returning to its usual slow, easy way. "We can't let this happen!"

They walked down the cul-de-sac, unmindful of the sun setting over the Pacific, creating an incredible sunset in the great masses of clouds that often hung on the horizon. Josh didn't even think that Kong might be lurking in the foliage along the fence.

"Start from the beginning," Josh suggested. "Tell me exactly what was said. Maybe that will give us a clue as to what we can do."

Haltingly, Tank recalled his and Marsha's conversation with their mother. She wouldn't lie to them, they knew, and they had asked questions that Mrs. Catlett wouldn't answer. Finally, Tank called his father at work, although personal calls were frowned upon by both parents and the corporation.

"Dad said that he and Mom were going to tell Marsha and me tonight, but because we had guessed that something was going on, he would go ahead and tell me. So he did—only now I wish he hadn't."

"Maybe he won't take the job," Josh said without conviction.

"He'll take it. I know my dad. He has until next Monday to notify the home office, but he'll take it because he really has no other choice."

"Where will it be in Alaska?" Josh wanted to know.

"Anchorage, Dad said."

Josh frowned. "I thought Juneau was the capital."

"It is, but Anchorage is ten times as big."

"Wish we had an atlas or encyclopedia," Josh mused. "I'd like to fix some of those places in my mind."

Tank kicked at a piece of coconut husk someone had left in the street. "It doesn't matter because I'm not going to go up there and leave you behind—not again."

Josh recognized the stubborn tone of his friend's voice, but it would take more than determination to keep Tank from moving away. Josh knew that both his and Tank's families were the kind that refused to be apart. As Mr. Ladd had often said, "Families belong together." Josh could see no way that the Catletts would let Tank stay behind.

"You say he's got to make a decision by next Monday?" Josh mused thoughtfully.

"That's what the company said, but Dad really has no choice but to move to Alaska."

"What does Marsha say?"

"She doesn't want to go either, but ... "

Josh interrupted, hope rising in his voice as a sudden idea came to him. "Your dad doesn't have to stay with the department store chain. He could stay right here in Honolulu and open his own business. That's what my dad did when he came here and decided to stay."

"Yeah!" Tank's face brightened. "Dad has worked in all departments: clothing, hardware, furniture. He knows enough about all those to have his own store."

Josh cautioned, "We need to think this through so that when we talk to your dad, he'll agree."

"Yeah! And you know who's the most akamai kid in the whole school? Manuel! Let's go ask him to help us!"

Dusk settled as Josh and Tank pushed open the sagging gate and took the short path toward Manuel's small house.

It sat high off the ground to discourage subterranean termites. The corrugated tin roof was rusted from hard seasonal rains.

"Hi!" Manuel greeted them from where he sat on the front porch. Good cooking smells drifted past him.

Josh and Tank returned the greeting, walking past banana trees rustling in the warm, gentle trade winds now heady with the sweet fragrance of plumeria* blossoms.

"We have a big problem and we need your super brain," Tank explained, stopping to lean against the wooden posts that supported the porch's tin roof.

Manuel's teeth flashed white in the gathering darkness. "You're in luck. I'm not charging my usual ten thousand dollars an hour for consultation."

Both Josh and Tank grinned and explained their situation in detail. When they had finished, Manuel stroked his chin as if deep in thought.

"Anchorage, you say?" he asked.

When both boys nodded, Manuel closed his eyes as though his computer brain worked better that way. "Makes sense, because the population there is around a quarter of a million people. The whole state has only about 600,000 population. Anchorage is not only Alaska's biggest city, it's the most cosmopolitan. The mos . . . "

"And probably the most ice and snow, with winters that last all year long!" Tank broke in angrily. "If we move there, there'll be no more beaches, no more sun, no more fun with Josh or you and Roger."

Tank's voice broke. He lowered his head quickly and looked unseeing toward the mountains, now black against the evening sky.

"What we need," Josh said quietly, "are some plans to help keep Tank's dad from moving up there. You have any suggestions?"

"Might have," Manuel replied. "The best thing, of course, is to persuade Mr. Catlett that it's more to his benefit to stay here than to move to Alaska."

"But how could we do that?" Josh asked doubtfully.

"Perhaps by convincing him that there are better opportunities here in Honolulu." Manuel paused as his mother called for him to wash for dinner.

"I have to go," he said, standing up. "But Mr. Catlett could leave the department store business and start his own business, be his own boss. That might appeal to him."

"We've already thought of that," Tank said, turning around again.

Manuel continued. "Also point out that it will cost a lot of money to move to Alaska. Besides, he'll have to buy entire new wardrobes for himself and the family. Warm clothes will cost a whole lot more than those we wear here in Hawaii. I hear it's very expensive up there—even more than Hawaii."

Josh and Tank exchanged nodding glances.

Manuel offered a couple of other possibilities. "Both of you go together and try to persuade him that it's to his advantage and that of his entire family to stay here with their friends. Then, Josh, you ask your father to intervene with Tank's dad."

Josh and Tank again nodded.

Manuel opened the screen door. "If all else fails, get your mother and sister to work on him, Tank. It's pretty hard for a man to stand against the women in his family. Josh, maybe your mother and Tiffany can also have a go at him."

Josh and Tank felt better as they hurried back to the apartment building, quickly setting up priorities for each of Manuel's suggestions.

***

Josh didn't think about Alicia until after he left Tank at his apartment and opened the door to his own.

The girls lay on the living room floor with a large atlas and a heavy encyclopedia open before them. Alicia looked at Josh, and he recalled her episode with Kong and Roger.

I should apologize to her, Josh told himself, remembering the look in her eyes when she mentioned losing her mother. Then Josh thought of how Alicia had humiliated Roger. He decided to wait with an apology.

"What are you two doing?" he asked, padding barefooted across the living room toward the kitchen. Before they could answer, he asked, "Mom, what's for dinner?"

"Mom's Surprise," she replied from the kitchen. That was her name for a dish made of leftovers and whatever else she had handy. "I was late getting home," she added.

"I had to fix something fast and easy."

Josh turned and looked at the girls. "Well?" he asked, referring to his last question to them.

Alicia replied with her own question. "Did you know that Alaska has the largest land mass of any of the fifty states?"

Josh didn't care, so he just shrugged.

Tiffany closed the encyclopedia on her finger to mark the page. "Alicia has told me an awful lot about Alaska. I sort of wish we were moving there, too."

Josh stifled a twinge of annoyance. He needed Tiffany to help convince the Catletts that they shouldn't leave Hawaii. He said, "Tank and I were talking before this all came up about how much we'd like to see Alaska, but that doesn't mean we want to move there. Fact is, Tank says he's not going."

"He's not?" Tiffany asked, sitting up in surprise.

"He doesn't want to, and I don't want him to either," Josh replied, flopping on the couch.

Mrs. Ladd stuck her head through the kitchen door. "What would he do instead?"

Josh thought quickly. "He could stay with us. You know, live here." He glanced around the apartment.

"That's silly!" Tiffany replied, her voice taking on the big-sister tone she sometimes used with both her younger brothers. "His parents wouldn't allow it, and even if they did, there's no room in this little apartment."

"He could share my room."

"It's Nathan's *and* your room," Mrs. Ladd reminded him, "and there's barely enough space in there for your little brother and you, especially the way you boys throw your clothes about and leave your things everywhere. Someday I'm going to get a bulldozer and go in there and clean up that room in spite of how you two would object."

Josh didn't think his and Nathan's bedroom was all that messy, but he didn't want to cause his mother to suggest he go clean it up. So Josh asked quickly, "Where is Nathan?"

"He's staying a few days with Chris, one of his friends from church," Mrs. Ladd replied. She returned to the kitchen, calling over her shoulder, "Tiffany, you'd better set the table. Josh, you'd better wash up. Your father will be home in a few minutes."

When Mr. Ladd arrived, Josh was alert for an opportunity to suggest he try talking Tank's father into staying in Hawaii. After the blessing, the food was passed, and everyone started eating.

Josh said, "Dad, Tank's father is probably moving to Alaska. Is that what you meant earlier today when we talked?"

His father nodded. "Yes, and I almost let the cat out of the bag. Anyway, we're all going to miss the Catletts, but it's a great opportunity for Sam."

Josh jumped in quickly. "Tank says he's not going."

Mr. Ladd looked sharply at his son, then narrowed his eyes knowingly. "I suppose that means you two are hatching some scheme for him to stay here."

Josh squirmed at his father's perception, but plunged ahead with his idea. "You could talk to Tank's dad about opening his own business here, as you did."

"You know I'm not going to interfere with Sam and Barbara's decisions."

"But Dad . . ."

Josh's father stopped him with a firm look, then followed it with one of his favorite ways of ending a discussion. "Have you and Tank prayed about this, son?"

The telephone rang, saving Josh from having to reply. As Mrs. Ladd answered on the kitchen phone, Josh thought, *I know what I want: for Tank and me not to be separated.* Josh wasn't eager to test to see if God's will was the same.

"It's for you, Josh," his mother said. "A Mr. Browning."

Josh took the phone and said hello.

The biologist said, "Since I hadn't heard from you, I thought I'd call to make sure you're still planning on coming to Kauai tomorrow."

"Yes, we are, but we haven't gotten our flight number and arrival time yet."

"When you get them, call me at my home phone number. I'll meet you at the airport with an enforcement officer. Then we'll see about catching those turtle poachers."

"Sounds great, Mr. Browning. You can count on Tank and me to do all we can to help."

When Josh hung up, he wondered briefly if this would be the last great adventure he and Tank would have together. *Must not think like that*, Josh scolded himself.

Looking across the table at Alicia, he remembered how she insisted on diving again where the shark had scared them. Between that, Tank's problem, and the threat of the poachers, Josh realized that tomorrow could be exciting and maybe even dangerous.

He didn't know how right he was.

Chapter Five

PART ALLIGATOR, PART GIRL

That night, Josh had mixed-up dreams. First, he saw himself scuba diving with Tiffany and Alicia. Tank had moved to Alaska, but Alicia had stayed in Hawaii. *I miss Tank*, Josh thought, sick at heart.

As before, a shark suddenly appeared in the clear waters and swam toward the unsuspecting girls. They were watching a small school of multicolored reef fish, their backs to the silent menace streaking toward them. This time it wasn't a harmless gray reef but a fourteen-foot tiger shark.

Josh tried to shout, but the words were muffled behind his regulator. Then, in the manner of dreams, the shark vanished and the two turtle poachers were chasing Josh. He was alone, and his pursuers were gaining. The haole gave a triumphant yell and grabbed Josh.

As Josh struggled to free himself, he thought, *If Tank were here, he'd help me, and everything would turn out all right. But he's moved, and I'll never see him again!*

Josh awoke, thrashing madly against the covering sheet, which had become entangled about him. Then he realized where he was and sat up, his heart racing.

He knew that Tank still lived downstairs, and they had a few days more in which to find a way to keep him from moving to Alaska with his family. *Got to hurry*, Josh reminded himself. *Must think of something.*

His thoughts jumped to Alicia. *I try to get along with everyone*, he thought as he freed himself from the sheet. *So why does she get under my skin?*

He pondered that as he got out of bed. He glanced at his little brother's empty bunk. Although Nathan sometimes slept over with Chris or with his other ten-year-old friends, Josh wished he were here just now. Josh wouldn't have felt so lonely.

He padded on bare feet to the louvered window, which opened toward Diamond Head. Daylight was sending silent fingers along its shadowed side. Near the peak, wild white pigeons called from the holes where they roosted. On a neighbor's lanai, little barred doves cooed greetings to the morning. Warm trade winds rustled the leaves on a slender rubber tree plant outside the window, then gently caressed the boy's cheeks.

It's so peaceful and beautiful here. Oh, why does Tank have to move away?

The emotional burdens of the day weighed Josh down as he dressed and went to the kitchen. His mother greeted him and announced that pancakes were almost ready. His sister was cutting a papaya* in half, and Alicia was pouring pink guava* juice into a glass pitcher.

After brief greetings, Alicia asked, "All ready for that dive today, Josh?"

He nodded without looking at her.

"You watch out for those turtle poachers," Alicia warned, setting the pitcher on the table, which was already set.

"They won't bother us with Mr. Browning around."

Mrs. Ladd slipped the last pancake onto the serving plate. "Breakfast is ready. Everyone, please sit down."

As they moved to obey, she added, "Josh, you know your father and I wouldn't give you permission to go back where those men chased you except that you'll be with the biologist and an enforcement officer from the DAR and whatever the rest of their agency is called."

"I know." The scary images of Josh's dream were already fading in the light of day. "Everything will be fine, Mom."

Before she could continue, Josh slid into his usual place at the breakfast nook. His sister and Alicia sat across from him. He hurriedly asked, "Where's Dad?"

"Alicia's father picked him up early."

Josh frowned. "Where did they go?"

Mrs. Ladd took her place at the end of the table nearest the range. "Mr. Wharton admires what your father has done with the paper, so they went down to see the early-morning press run. They'll be back shortly. Now, everyone please hold hands while I say the blessing."

After breakfast, Josh went downstairs to see if Tank had

had any success in talking his father out of moving to Alaska. Tank came outside in answer to Josh's call.

"How'd it go with your dad?" Josh asked.

"Terrible! I struck out. My sister isn't much help. She seemed to like the idea of Alaska."

The bad news caused both boys to fall silent until Tiffany and Alicia stepped onto the lanai to watch for Kapali. He was expected to arrive any minute to drive them to the airport for the flight to Lihue.

Tank glared up at Alicia as she chatted with Tiffany. "I hope she doesn't get us into any trouble today. I don't feel like hassling with her."

"Remember, we've got to be nice to her."

"I'll be nice to her," Tank muttered. "But if I get a chance ... "

He left his sentence unfinished as a car moved up the cul-de-sac. "That doesn't look like the one Kapali was driving yesterday," Tank mused.

"It's my dad and Mr. Wharton."

Alicia's father slowed the rental car as it came abreast of the boys.

After everyone exchanged pleasantries, Mr. Wharton said with a smile, "You kids have fun today, but be careful. Understand?"

They nodded while Josh studied the man. He was in his mid-forties, of medium height, with sandy hair and steely gray eyes that seemed to see everything. He had a casual, unpolished air about him, but Josh knew that anyone who was an Alaskan bush pilot had to be competent, self-reliant, and familiar with great risks.

"Thanks for being so good to Alicia," her father continued as she and Tiffany left the lanai to come downstairs.

Josh didn't reply, but Tank muttered something unintelligible. Josh discreetly jabbed him in the ribs.

As Tiffany and Alicia stopped outside the apartment door to put on their shoes, Mr. Wharton added, "You know, boys, Alicia is quite a girl." He shook his head and added ruefully, "Actually, she's still more tomboy than girl, but she'll grow out of that. Down where I was raised before moving to Alaska, we'd say Alicia is part alligator and part girl."

Josh heard Tank make a low strangled sound.

Mr. Wharton watched the girls start down the outside stairs, then looked at Tank. "You're going to have the greatest time of your life in Alaska. Alicia and I will fly you into places that have no roads. We'll land on glaciers and lakes and in places most people would give their eyeteeth to see. You'll also catch the biggest fish you've ever seen and see great bears and huge moose up close."

Josh found himself getting excited. He remembered how he and Tank had talked earlier about the great adventures they could have in Alaska. But neither had guessed they would really go there. They certainly had not dreamed that Tank would go alone, leaving Josh behind in Hawaii.

Mr. Wharton concluded, "Yes sirree, Tank, you're in for a real treat!"

"I don't want to go to Alaska," Tank said stubbornly, thrusting out his chin. "I like it here."

Tiffany and Alicia reached the car in time to hear that remark. Alicia leaned through the open driver's side window and gave her father a quick kiss on the cheek before turning to Tank.

"You'll get over that," Alicia said. "In fact, you'll wonder why you ever wanted to live in Hawaii."

"She's right, Tank," Mr. Wharton assured him. "Why, the way you love adventure, you'll have a ball. The best part of it is, it can happen when you least expect it."

"That's right," Alicia added. "Dad, remember when we were having a picnic just outside of town, and those two big old grizzly bears waltzed in, bold as you please?"

Her father smiled and nodded. "They were between me and my rifle, which was leaning against a tree. Of course, I had my .357 Magnum handgun strapped on, and that's a mighty powerful weapon. But it wouldn't have been much use against those bears if they'd decided to turn on us."

In spite of himself, Josh asked, "What happened?"

Mr. Wharton chuckled. "Nothing, really. The bears just helped themselves to our lunches and walked off."

"Sort of like that shark the other day," Alicia said to the boys. "Nothing really happened."

"Shark?" Mr. Wharton asked. "Did you tangle with a shark, Alicia?"

"It wasn't anything, Daddy. I'll tell you later."

Behind him, Josh heard Tank mimic Alicia under his

breath so only Josh could hear. "*It wasn't anything*. Oh, no! She just almost got us eaten alive, that's all."

Alicia's father asked, "What was that, Tank?"

"Uh . . . nothing."

Mr. Wharton nodded. "Well, see all of you later."

As the car moved on, the boys walked a few steps away from the girls.

"She's more alligator than girl, if you ask me," Tank grumbled. When Josh didn't answer, Tank continued. "But we have more important things to think about. Like, how are we going to keep my dad from moving away, not to mention what could happen today with the dive and the poachers?"

Josh nodded absently. "We sure do. But I'm kind of curious about Mr. Wharton. Maybe I can get Alicia to tell me about him on the flight to Kauai."

On the short hop to the neighboring island, Alicia talked freely about her father, Trent Wharton. After serving as a gunner on a gunship during the Vietnam War*, he had come home restless. He started drifting and ended up in Alaska, where he became a bush pilot and a businessman. Now well-to-do, he owned three float planes and operated several lodges in different parts of the forty-ninth state. He knew everybody, from the governor on down.

Alicia paused, then added softly, "Dad met my mother while piloting her and her father to a glacier. They married and had me. She died two years ago of cancer."

"I'm sorry," Josh said. Whatever he thought of Alicia,

no kid should have a parent die.

Alicia fell silent a moment, then turned to Tank. "Dad and I meant what we said a little while ago. Why, the way you love adventure, you'll be absolutely fascinated with Alaska."

"It won't be any fun without Josh," Tank said stoutly.

"You'll have me," Alicia replied.

Tank's lip curled slightly. "Girls can't have fun and adventures like boys."

"Is that so?" Alicia snapped. "Let me tell you something, Mr. Tank Catlett! I'm just as adventuresome as you and Josh. Maybe even more so. I can already fly a plane, although I can't solo. Can you?"

"Well, no . . . ," Tank began, but she cut him off.

"Can you survive in icy waters if your plane goes down?" Alicia demanded hotly. Without waiting for an answer, she continued. "I have. I've also faced a mad moose on a trail with nothing in my hands. And once I unexpectedly came upon a mother grizzly with cubs and lived to tell about it. Could you have done the same?"

Tiffany acted as peacemaker. "Aw, come on, you two. Let's just have fun today. Okay?"

There was no more wrangling, but the tension was still great when they landed on Kauai, where Gary Browning and another man met them. Both were in plain clothes, but Josh noticed the enforcement officer carried a badge.

Mr. Browning, wearing long tan pants and an aloha shirt*, was a big haole with a warm smile and hearty handshake. He introduced his shorter, slightly balding companion as Jeff Kimura, a Japanese-American. He wore shorts and a faded old aloha shirt that almost concealed the gun on his hip.

When introductions were completed, Mr. Browning announced, "We came in an unmarked four-wheel-drive vehicle. We don't want to appear too conspicuous if those poachers are still around. Now, let's see where you boys found that carcass."

Following Kapali's directions, the biologist drove down the bumpy dirt road in the sugarcane field to where Kapali had parked his Jeep earlier in the week. From there they walked, carrying the diving gear. They carefully picked their way past the ironwood trees and the slippery needles that had fallen to the ground.

Josh and Tank pointed out where they had been when they first saw the poachers and then where they had found the carcass. Finally, the boys showed where they had been chased and repelled their attackers with rocks.

"You've been very helpful," Mr. Browning said. "I'll join Jeff in scouting around. Maybe we can find something that will help us apprehend those poachers."

"Could Tank and I help?" Josh asked.

"No, thanks. You go on and enjoy your dive."

The two men from the Division of Aquatic Resources began their slow search. Josh and the others walked back to where they had the experience with the shark. Kapali again stayed in the boat while the girls and boys dived.

The clear, relaxing waters soothed Josh's jangled nerves. He had unsuccessfully tried not to think about Tank moving away, but there was something so peaceful about Hawaii underwater that slowly Josh's painful thoughts melted away.

Both he and Tank had been quite sure there would be no repeat of the earlier shark incident because the dive shop had assured them that all four regulators were in fine working order. However, Josh was still cautious, keeping keenly alert as last night's dream faded.

A turtle about three feet long swam by, looking, Josh thought, like a floating trash-can lid. He was surprised when Alicia started swimming after the turtle. She caught up with it, grabbed the top of the shell, and hung on as the startled creature took off.

Josh swam as fast as he could and seized Alicia by her right ankle just above the flipper. He pulled her off, and the turtle quickly swam away. Alicia whirled to face Josh, her eyes angry behind her mask. She jerked her thumb up, signaling that they should surface. Josh nodded and followed her toward the sunlight.

As they broke the surface, Alicia snatched the regulator from her mouth and shoved the mask up on her forehead. "Why did you do that?" she demanded hotly.

Josh removed the regulator from his mouth and forced himself to explain calmly. "Because it's against the law to bother a sea turtle—even ride on one."

"I wasn't hurting it. I was just having fun!"

"The turtle wasn't," Josh answered quietly. "It was scared. That's why it took off so fast."

Alicia opened her mouth as if to make another sharp remark but stopped and smiled at Josh. "Forget it," she said. "After all, I did what I came for: got back on the horse that threw me. I'm not afraid to dive again."

Josh nodded, eager to again ease the tension that Alicia seemed to generate. "Good," he said. "I think I'll go ashore to see what Mr. Browning and Mr. Kimura found."

"Me, too," declared Tank, who had followed them up.

Everyone loaded their equipment into the boat, and Kapali took them back to land.

Mr. Browning and Mr. Kimura were waiting for them. Josh asked if they had found anything.

"Not really," Mr. Browning replied, "although there were some fresh footprints and a place where a boat had been pulled up on the shore."

"So the poachers are still around?" Josh asked.

"Looks that way," Mr. Kimura agreed. "You kids see any turtles?"

Josh glanced at Alicia and said, "Only one."

"I tried to ride it," Alicia volunteered, "but Josh pulled me off real fast. He told me that it's against the law, but I didn't know that."

Both men nodded, and Mr. Kimura said, "Now you do. But remember, young lady, if I had seen you do that, you'd be in trouble."

"I won't do it again," she promised.

Josh picked up his gear and started following the two men back toward their vehicle. *At least she's honest*, Josh grudgingly admitted. *Give her credit for that.*

Alicia picked her way across the treacherous ironwood needles. "Josh, it's too bad you and Tank didn't get a chance to chase those men who killed the turtle. With Mr. Browning, Mr. Kimura, and Kapali to help, those poachers could be on their way to jail."

"I guess they're not around today," Josh replied.

"Yeah," Tank said. "The way I'm feeling about having to move to Alaska, I would have really loved to run into those guys. Chasing them would give me some way to work off part of my frustration."

"There will be another time," Mr. Browning assured them. "We'll catch them sooner or later."

They had reached the vehicle and were starting to put their gear inside when Josh pointed to the windshield. "What's that under the wiper blade?"

Mr. Browning replied, "I'll find out." He and Mr. Kimura moved to the front of the vehicle where Mr. Browning removed a small, torn piece of paper.

As Josh and the others crowded about, Mr. Browning read aloud: "Stay away from here if you don't want to end up like that turtle."

Chapter Six

WHEN PLANS GO WRONG

Mr. Kimura took the threatening note from Mr. Browning, folded it, and put it in his shirt pocket. "I'll take this to the office for analysis, then do a follow-up investigation."

Josh said, "Since this is the second time we know the poachers have been here, maybe they live nearby."

"They probably do live someplace close," Mr. Browning replied, sliding behind the steering wheel. "But wherever they live, we'll catch them sooner or later."

"Yeah!" Tank said, watching the girls get into the vehicle. "And when you do, Josh and I would like to help, wouldn't we?"

"Sure would," Josh agreed, putting his diving equipment into the vehicle, "but I don't know when we'll be back here."

Tiffany settled into her seat beside Alicia. "Maybe Dad would like to do an article about the turtles, and we could come with him."

"That's possible," Josh replied. "Mr. Browning, our dad owns a tourist newspaper in Waikiki. Maybe he could run a story with pictures that would help other people be on the lookout for the poachers."

Alicia asked scornfully, "Who's going to read a Waikiki tourist publication on this island?"

Josh patiently explained. "Lots of people bring Dad's paper with them to all the islands. Besides, it's also distributed here on Kauai."

Mr. Browning started the motor. "Shining a light in dark places is always a good idea. The media do that. What do you think, Jeff?"

The enforcement officer nodded. "Wouldn't hurt."

Tank grinned at Josh. "It will also give us another chance to come back here and catch the poachers."

Mr. Browning added, "I like that idea so much that I'll call the daily newspapers, too."

On the flight back to Honolulu, Josh and Tank made plans for that evening. They would try talking to Mr. Catlett in the hope of changing his mind about Alaska.

That evening, Tiffany and Alicia went to see a film at a Waikiki theater. While waiting for Tank to call saying his father was home, Josh unsuccessfully tried to phone Roger. In a sad voice, Mrs. Okamoto informed Josh that Roger was in his room and didn't want to be disturbed.

She went on to explain that Roger didn't want to talk to anyone. He was still embarrassed over the girl from Alaska saving him from Kong. Josh asked Mrs. Okamoto to say he had called. Josh sympathized with Roger and wondered how to help him.

The least Alicia can do, Josh told himself, *is apologize to Roger. But if he won't speak to me, I'm sure that he won't talk to her.*

As Josh started to turn away from the phone, it rang. He picked it up to hear Tank say briefly, "Dad's home. Come on down."

With a silent prayer that Tank and he would not have to be separated, Josh hurried down the stairs. Tank's father looked up from where he was studying a map of Alaska. *That looks bad*, Josh thought.

Sam Catlett was slender, wiry, and in his late thirties. He had loosened his tie and taken off his coat, but still had on the lightweight blue suit pants he had worn to work that day. His blond hair was perfectly styled, with every hair in place.

"Evening, Josh," he said. "How are you and Alicia getting along?"

Josh shrugged. "Okay, I guess."

Mr. Catlett smiled. "Your sister told my daughter some of the experiences Alicia has put you boys through. I guess she's quite a handful."

"Her own father said she's part alligator and part girl." Josh hoped that summarized his feelings, except he secretly agreed with Tank's earlier remark that Alicia seemed mostly alligator.

"I suppose," Mr. Catlett said, motioning for the boys to

sit down, "that as long as you and Tank have been friends, an aggressive tomboy like Alicia can be quite annoying to be around."

Tank snorted. "She certainly can!"

Josh saw a way to ease into the reason he and Tank were there. "Twelve years. That's how long Tank and I have been best friends."

"Oh, yes. Since you were babies...." Mr. Catlett let his voice trail off. His gray eyes narrowed slightly. "I think I know why you boys are here together. You don't want Tank to move to Alaska. Is that it?"

When both boys nodded vigorously, Tank's father continued. "I know how hard it must be for you both to think about being separated if I take the position in Alaska."

"If?" Tank jumped at the word. "That means you haven't yet made up your mind."

"Not yet, but your mother and I are leaning that way. I think we're gradually convincing your sister."

Josh saw the light of hope fade in his friend's eyes. "Mr. Catlett," Josh began, "have you ever thought about staying here in Honolulu and maybe opening your own store? Being your own boss?"

"This far from the home office, I am pretty much my own boss. Of course, the top store officers come here every chance they get. But they say only enough to me to be able to write the trip off on their income taxes. Then they go have fun—go sight-seeing and so forth. This store has made a nice profit since I came, so they don't really bother me."

Josh saw his plan wasn't working, so he shifted his approach. "As the manager, you get a bonus or something if your store does well, don't you?"

"There are perks*, of course. Why do you ask?"

"Alaska has far fewer people than Hawaii, so by comparison, a store up there couldn't possibly make as much money as this one does. So you'd make less, too, wouldn't you?"

Mr. Catlett smiled knowingly. "That's an astute observation, Josh, but I've never worked for money alone. I love a challenge. The Anchorage store would certainly offer that. That appeals to me more than the money, although I expect to do quite well there financially."

Josh's hopes sank. "It sounds as though you've already made up your mind to move, Mr. Catlett."

"Maybe I have."

Tank groaned in despair and flopped his arms out over the back of the couch.

Josh tried to use all the reasons that Manuel had suggested. "But Mr. Catlett," Josh said earnestly, "it will cost you an awful lot to move. The cost of clothing will be higher—and maybe housing, too."

"The company will pay moving expenses, and I get an employee discount at the store, so clothing won't be a problem for my family."

Josh felt desperate. He tried another possibility. "If you do move there, could I go, too, and live with Tank?"

Mr. Catlett leaned forward, his face serious. "Josh, I

know how very, very much you and Tank want to stay together. But your parents wouldn't allow that."

Tank regained his composure to pounce on an opening. "Then how about letting me stay with Josh?"

Mr. Catlett took a slow, deep breath and then blew it out before answering. "Tank, even if John and Mary had room—which they don't—and even if they were willing to take you in, we Catletts are a family. We must stay together. I hope you understand. And you, too, Josh."

With an aching heart, Josh looked at his friend.

Tank licked his lips and blinked rapidly. "Excuse me," he cried as he leaped up and hurried down the hallway toward his bedroom.

Josh stared helplessly after him. Then, in defeat, he said good night to Mr. Catlett and walked out into the night. *That's it*, Josh told himself with a mixture of pain and anger. *If Marsha is shifting over to her mother and father's side, what else can Tank and I do?*

He started up the outside stairs, then paused and looked back at Diamond Head's massive hulk rising against the cloudless sky. *But I'm not going to give up. Somehow there's got to be a way for Tank and me to stay together.*

Josh reentered his family's apartment. His father lowered the newspaper he was reading and looked over the top of his silver-framed half glasses.

"What's the matter, son?"

"I just talked to Tank's father. I think he's going to take the store in Alaska."

Mr. Ladd laid his paper down on his lap and patted the chair beside him. "Sit down. Let me see if I can explain something to you."

Josh sat, saying miserably, "I realize that it's a fact of life that sooner or later everybody gets parted. But I don't want to be away from Tank. It was bad enough when he moved to Hawaii while we were still in Los Angeles. But to move to Alaska . . . "

"Alaska has its good points, son."

Josh recognized the finality of his father's tone. Tank and Josh had lost again. Aloud, Josh said, "Dad, if you don't mind, I don't want to talk about it, okay?"

"Very well. But talking about problems is a good way to help work through them."

Josh changed the subject. "Where is everybody?"

"Your mother and Barbara Catlett went to some kind of a women's doings at the church. Your sister and Alicia are at a movie. Nathan is still staying at Chris's house. So you and I are alone. I'm in a listening mood if you want to talk."

Josh realized this was a good time to ask about something that bothered him. "Dad, how come you're spending so much time with Alicia's father?"

"Several reasons. I like him. He's a very interesting man. He started with nothing and has become a highly successful businessman. I only recently started in business, so I can learn a lot from him."

"What does he know about tourist publications?"

"Nothing, but good business principles often are applicable to more than one enterprise. He says he's learning from me, too, because I left teaching high school history and am making a profit in publishing. He's interested in how I did it, and I want to hear his ideas on how to improve my profits. So it's a mutual relationship with Trent."

Josh's vague sense of uneasiness softened, but he asked one final question. "You're not thinking of selling out to him, are you, Dad?"

He chuckled. "Absolutely not!"

Satisfied, Josh turned the conversation to the biologist's offer to show them a sea-turtle nesting site. "He said you can take pictures as long as you don't tell where the nests are. You want to go?"

"Of course, son. It sounds like a wonderful idea." He tapped the newspaper he had been reading. "There's a story in here about the carcasses that have been found. Authorities are asking citizens to call in if they have information that will help catch the poachers."

Josh wanted to say that he and Tank had that as their goal. Instead, Josh told about being chased after the encounter with the shark and finding the warning note yesterday.

"You boys had better stay away from that place," Mr. Ladd said firmly. "Let the authorities handle it."

Josh didn't want to hear that, but he recognized that his father's counsel was probably wise. Josh promised,

"We won't go there unless we're with Mr. Browning or Mr. Kimura."

His father nodded approval. Just then, Tiffany and Alicia arrived at the door.

Tiffany exclaimed, "Dad! Josh! We saw a great film!"

"It was about this whale," Alicia explained. "There was a girl who swam with them. . . ." She broke off, noticing Josh's long face. "Look," she said defensively, "if you're looking so unhappy because I embarrassed your friend Roger . . ."

"It's not just that," Josh interrupted, but he decided not to elaborate.

Alicia shrugged. "Well, I've got to run. Kapali is waiting to drive me back to the hotel." At the door, she turned to look at Josh.

"Tiffany and I were talking on the ride back from the film. She said that people can watch whales passing off-shore of Hawaii."

"That's true," Josh admitted. "But it's pretty late in the year for them. Most of the migration is over."

Mr. Ladd spoke up. "Not quite, son. There's a piece in today's paper about some humpbacks being spotted off-shore yesterday. Apparently, they're mostly mothers with calves. They have to travel more slowly."

"Fantastic!" Alicia exclaimed. "I'd love to see a baby whale! I'll have Kapali make arrangements for us to go out on a boat so we can see the whales up close. Well, see you about eight tomorrow morning."

"Can't tomorrow," Josh said quickly. "Dad and I are going to Maui with Tank."

Alicia hesitated a moment, thinking. "That's okay, because there are some girl things Tiffany and I want to do. You guys have fun, and we'll go whale watching the day after. Bye."

She was out the door before Josh could protest to her, but he turned to his sister. "I don't want to go whale watching. Besides, Mr. Browning is supposed to call about taking Dad to see the turtle nesting areas."

"What you mean is that you're not crazy about going with Alicia because she might get us into trouble again."

"You've got to admit she's done plenty of that."

"Well, I'm beginning to like her more and more, but we can't go off with the driver without you and Tank."

"She's right, son," Mr. Ladd said. "The four of you young people need to stay together. Besides, Alicia is our guest. She'll be here only a few more days. We owe her the courtesy of doing all we can to make her visit pleasant."

"But Dad, she's sort of reckless! She's always doing dumb things. And she's also so stubborn! She won't listen to anybody. She does what she pleases. Her father has spoiled her. . . ."

"Enough, son!" Josh's father's voice was stern. "We are not to be judgmental. Now, I suggest you call Tank and tell him we're leaving early tomorrow for Maui."

Josh had always enjoyed the second largest of the main Hawaiian islands, and especially the old whaling port of

Lahaina*. But the trip the next day turned out to be uneventful because Tank was feeling gloomy. Except for renting jet skis at Lahaina and riding them for an hour, the boys just walked around the historic old town where missionaries and whaleboat men had once clashed over how to treat the native Hawaiians. Josh was glad when the day ended and he flew home with his father and Tank.

The following morning, Kapali drove Josh, Tank, Tiffany, and Alicia to where they could watch whales. They eased down a dirt road that was little more than a couple of tracks through thorny kiawe* trees. After a short, bouncy ride, they came upon a small board-and-batten house with a rusted corrugated metal roof, located near the water's edge.

"My friend's place," Kapali explained. "I'll go tell him we're here and get the key. Meet you kids down there by the boat."

Josh was familiar with the vessel called a Boston Whaler. He and the others had donned life preservers when Kapali returned.

"My friend said he saw a pod of whales blowing just a few minutes ago. They swim only about three to eight miles an hour. We should quickly catch up to them."

Josh began to feel excited about the prospect of seeing the largest mammals on earth up close. At Alicia's urging, Kapali, who usually didn't say much, told briefly about the whales.

"They swim three thousand miles of open ocean to breed here because Hawaii's waters are so warm. Later, they return to the polar regions where they started. They grow up to about eighty feet and weigh maybe eighty thousand pounds. They can . . . there! See the spout?"

Josh saw it first: a spray of water about twenty feet high. Then he saw the gray-black whale. At once a smaller spout shot up.

"A baby whale!" Alicia cried. "A mother and baby! Oh, Kapali, take us in close!"

"I'll ease off on the power," he replied, "but everyone look around real carefully. Sometimes a male escorts the cow."

Everyone looked around carefully, but saw no other spouting or sign of another whale.

"Doesn't mean one isn't there," Kapali warned. "They can stay underwater for up to forty-five minutes."

Everyone fell silent as they watched the cow and calf make only shallow dives and then resurface as the boat crept closer. At last Kapali cut the motor and let the boat's momentum carry them alongside the seventy-foot-long mother and her calf.

"Oh," Alicia whispered, "they're so beautiful! Like in the movie last night when the girl swam with . . . "

Alicia let her voice trail off, causing Josh to look up in sudden alarm. Alicia quickly pulled off her muumuu*, showing her bathing suit beneath.

Josh realized what she was going to do. "No! Don't!" he cried.

Alicia ignored him, sliding quietly over the side not ten

feet from the mother and calf.

At the same instant, through the clear water below, Josh saw something long and black shooting up from the depths. He shouted, "Alicia! Look out!"

It was too late. She had dived beneath the surface.

Chapter Seven

SWIMMING WITH WHALES

For a second Josh stood in shock, fascinated by what looked like a giant submarine surfacing rapidly. Then he realized it was another whale shooting up from the Pacific's depths.

Kapali cried, "It's a male escort!" He started the motor. "Hang on, everyone! You boys reach out and grab Alicia when I run past her. We'll get only one chance, so don't miss!"

The boys obeyed, crouching over the sides as the motor roared to life.

Tank shouted, "She's going to get hurt!"

"Brace yourself," Josh called back. "Let's not get pulled overboard when we grab her!"

From behind Josh, his sister pointed and screamed. "We're too late!"

Josh gulped and involuntarily drew back as the monstrous escort shot out of the water, breaking the surface between the girl and the other whales. The escort didn't touch Alicia, but the turbulent water rushing by his body tumbled her aside as he leaped high into the air. It seemed a third of his great body was clear of the water before he slowed.

"Look out!" Josh yelled to Alicia. "He's going to crash back down . . . !"

The words were drowned out as the escort whale's great leap ended and he fell back with a mighty splash. The waves rocked the boat so violently that Josh grabbed for the sides and hung on. He fearfully watched the big whale dive beneath the water and yelled a warning: "He'll probably do that again!"

Josh felt the boat slow as it came alongside Alicia. Her face was pale and her eyes wide with fright as Josh and Tank reached out to her.

"Hold out your hands!" Josh shouted to Alicia.

She reach up frantically. Josh grabbed her right arm and braced himself. Out of the corner of his eye, he saw Tank grab Alicia's other arm.

"Pull, Tank, pull!" Josh yelled, straining backward.

Alicia was dragged headfirst across the side of the boat. She cried out in pain before flopping like a big fish on the boat's flat bottom.

Tank yelled furiously, "What's the matter with you, Alicia? That was the dumbest . . . !"

"Hang on!" Kapali shouted, pointing over the side. "The male's going to make another pass at us!"

Josh looked up in alarm just as Kapali opened the

throttle wide, making the engine roar. Josh glimpsed the mother whale and her calf swimming leisurely away, but the escort wasn't in sight.

When Kapali suddenly turned the boat sharply to the left, Josh saw with horror that the huge escort whale was again shooting for the surface just ahead of them. Josh grabbed a firm hold on the boat's side and shot a frightened glance over the water.

Both girls screamed as the male again breached, leaping high into the air and sending a wall of foaming water over the boat's bow. But this time the great beast did not dive. He stretched his huge length out and landed fairly flat, like a boy taking a gigantic belly flop.

Josh watched in silent fascination as the whale arched his back and nosed downward, making the flukes* on his wide tail rise slowly and ponderously from the water.

Tank yelled, "He's going to smash the boat!"

Both girls shrieked, and Josh watched helplessly as the tail flattened out and started to slap down on the boat's bow.

"It's going to hit us!" Josh cried just as he felt the boat swerve sharply again.

The whale's tail crashed down explosively, missing the bow by inches. This was followed by a huge wave that passed underneath the boat, lifting the motor out of the water. Josh heard the propeller spinning in the air and the motor racing. Then the boat dropped back into the sea with such force that Josh was nearly thrown overboard.

Josh swiveled around to look back. All three whales

were swimming leisurely away. The male was between the boat and the other two whales. He seemed to be herding them to safety.

Kapali cut the motor, and everyone watched the great mammals as they sounded. A sudden silence settled over everyone.

Josh asked Kapali, "You think they'll come back?"

"I don't think so. I believe that big fellow feels he has taught us humans a lesson."

"Wow!" Alicia exclaimed, clapping her hands like a delighted child. "Wasn't that something?"

Josh and Tank spun around to face her.

Tank yelled angrily, "You almost got us killed! If his tail had hit this boat . . . !"

"Easy, Tank," Josh interrupted, although his adrenaline was pumping and he was so angry he also wanted to shout at Alicia. He forced himself to ask calmly, "Are you hurt?"

She glanced over her body. "No, except I'm a little scratched up, but I don't know if that's from the barnacles on the whale's side or from where you two guys dragged me into the boat."

Kapali eased off on the throttle so his voice could be heard above the motor. "That big whale didn't mean to hurt you, I'm sure. He just wanted you to know that you weren't wanted in his territory."

Josh had some difficulty keeping Tank from exploding as the boat headed for shore. Josh also struggled with his own emotions. He bitterly asked himself, *When am I going to learn to tell her no? Just because Dad says I've got to be nice to her doesn't mean I have to let her get the rest of us into trouble. But I'm afraid if I say anything, I'll blow up and say something that I'll be sorry about later.*

Nobody felt like swimming, so Kapali said he would drive up the coast toward Makaha*, saying they would later return through the center of the island. They all crawled into the car, and the girls began talking quietly between themselves, but Josh and Tank rode in tense silence.

Finally, Josh leaned toward his friend and said in a low voice, "That did it. I'm not going to let her talk us into going anywhere that's dangerous, even if she does get mad and my father grounds me."

"Me, too. No sense in letting her get us killed."

Josh nodded. "You and I do lots of exciting things, but we're not foolish. Alicia is. She scares me."

Kapali asked, "You kids ever seen the Witch's Cauldron?"

The girls shook their heads. Alicia asked, "What is it?"

"I'll show you." Kapali slowed and headed northeast on the Farrington Highway, State Route 93.

Josh said, "I think I've heard of it. Kapali, isn't that where there's a sort of cave in the shore, and the water rushes in, then back out, making the place in front of the cave full of whirlpools?"

"That's it," the driver admitted. "The wildest water you ever saw in such a small place. People sometimes get careless and stand too close above it. A big wave can come along and sweep them off."

"So we'll all be extra careful," Tiffany said.

Josh suggested, "Why don't we just stay in the car and look at it from a distance?" He avoided making eye contact with Alicia, fearing she would know he was thinking of her capacity for getting them into trouble.

The others agreed.

Soon they drove past some older boys riding jet skis off a small stretch of beach. A few hundred yards beyond that, Kapali stopped the car and pointed. "There it is. See why it's called the Witch's Cauldron?"

Josh's blue eyes swept over one of the most incredible sights he had ever seen in all his adventures.

A narrow natural channel of ancient coral reefs led inland from the ocean about a hundred feet. Waves hitting the reefs leaped high and then collapsed thunderously. In the shallows, the water gathered speed, hurtling toward land.

The waves poured violently into a small opening that further narrowed to a channel about sixty feet wide. Forced into this confined area, the water continued to gain speed until it entered a round natural basin or cauldron, where two separate actions occurred simultaneously. Part of the water began to whirl violently, racing around the confining bowl, boiling furiously and turning the entire surface white with foam. At the same time, the central stream of incoming water from the channel shot straight ahead through the turbulent basin and hurled itself against the far end of the cauldron.

Countless years of such furious assaults had hollowed out a twenty-foot-deep cavern that had probably started as part of an ancient lava tube*. Only the top half of the cave's mouth showed. As the water plunged violently into the cave, the air inside was forced out with a groan. The cave disappeared in a swirl of wild, foaming water. A couple of large waves sloshed over the top where the cave had been, spreading over the bald volcanic dome on land.

After about twenty seconds, the water retreated, draining from the land and rushing out of the cave. The top of the cave's mouth reappeared through the frothy cascade. The turbulent water in the basin started moving seaward toward the channel. The retreat was blocked by the next incoming tidal surge, which repeated the whole process.

No one said anything as they gazed on the awesome sight. Finally, Kapali spoke. "My father told me that when he was a young man, he helped save somebody who got swept into that cave. Still happens sometimes, but usually when somebody gets in that place, they drown."

Josh didn't doubt that sobering statement. He glanced down the beach a short distance where the jet skis roared along in the safe water.

Tiffany shuddered. "Do you mind if we go on? I'm scared just to look at this place."

Alicia protested. "In a minute! I want to walk up for a closer look."

"No!" Josh heard himself say firmly as he reached out to stop the girl's hand from grasping the door handle.

Alicia turned on him with eyes suddenly blazing. "Just who do you think you are, telling me . . . ?"

Kapali interrupted. "Excuse me, young lady, but Josh is right. Why take a chance?"

Alicia turned on him. "You're not bossing me!"

Tiffany spoke quickly but firmly. "Listen, Alicia! I like you, but I'm with Josh and Kapali in this."

"And me!" Tank said fervently.

Alicia hesitated, and Josh asked quietly, "Why don't we all forget about this place and go home?"

Alicia shrugged. "Oh, all right, I guess."

***

That night, Josh and Tank sat on the Catletts' ground-floor lanai and looked up at Diamond Head with the moon sailing above it.

"I'm still scared, thinking about what could have happened if Alicia had insisted on going to that Witch's Cauldron," Josh said. "I can hardly wait for her to go home."

"Yeah. Just four more days. But unless you and I come up with some plan to stop my dad from moving to Alaska, you'll be rid of her, but she could be my neighbor up there. We can't let that happen."

"We've tried everything we could think of, plus what Manuel suggested." Josh started naming them. "We tried persuading your dad that it's to his benefit to stay here instead of moving to Alaska. We tried to show him that there are better opportunities here in Hawaii."

"Yeah!" Tank took up the recounting. "Dad didn't want to leave the department store and start his own business. He said he was already pretty much his own boss. We talked about the cost of moving and buying heavy clothes and the cost of living up there."

"We tried to get your parents to let you live with me. My dad said no, and when we tried to get your father to let me live with you, he said no. And my dad refused to interfere with your folks' decision."

Tank sighed heavily. "That's everything, and nothing has worked."

"You're forgetting Manuel's final suggestion. Remember, he said if all else fails, get the women and girls to work on him."

Tank's tone lightened. "Yeah! He said it's pretty hard for a man to stand against his wife and daughter." Tank paused, then continued. "But my sister is starting to like the idea of Alaska, and Mom says she'll go wherever Dad does. That leaves only your mom ... "

"She already told me no," Josh broke in. "But we just can't give up!"

"I know. What are we overlooking?"

Josh remembered that his father had suggested praying about God's will in this matter. But Josh hadn't done that, and he decided not to mention it now.

Both boys fell silent as headlights moved up the cul-de-sac. The vehicle stopped in front of the apartment building, and Roger got out.

Tank called over the railing, "Hey, Roger! Come talk to us awhile."

"Can't," Roger replied, closing the car door and hurrying toward the outside stairs.

Tank asked Josh, "How do you like this? We're his friends, and we didn't have anything to do with Alicia humiliating Roger with Kong."

Josh didn't answer until the car turned around and followed its headlights back down the street. "Did you see the sign on the side of the car door when he closed it?"

"No. Why?"

"It said Karate School. Do you think ... ?"

"Wouldn't do any good," Tank interrupted. "By the time Roger even learns how to assume the right defensive stance, Kong will have beaten up on him several times. That is, if he can catch Roger alone again."

"Not much chance of that. We don't even get to see Roger anymore. But I'll tell you, Roger is fast and he's strong. If he came at me with his hands up in that karate way, I'd back off real fast, and I'm bigger than he is."

"But nobody is as big as Kong," Tank reminded him.

"That's a fact," Josh agreed, standing up. "Well, I'd better get upstairs and see what Dad found out about going to Kauai to take pictures of turtle nesting sites."

Josh met his sister and Alicia coming down the stairs.

"If it'll make you feel better," Alicia told him as they passed, "I tried to apologize to Roger just now, but he wouldn't let me."

"You did?" Josh's surprise was genuine.

"Yes. I tried phoning before that, but his mother said he wouldn't talk to me. So later I knocked at his apartment door, but his mother said that he wasn't home. I met him coming upstairs just now, but he wouldn't even stop. So I don't know what else I can do to help him get over being hurt because of what happened with Kong."

"I don't either," Josh admitted.

As he unlocked the apartment door, Josh had mixed feelings about Alicia. Earlier he had been very angry with her. She still was a royal pain, he decided, but she had a good side, too.

Still, Josh told himself, *it will be great when she leaves in a few days.* He immediately shook his head. *No, it won't be great, because Tank will probably be getting ready to move away.*

Mr. Ladd was reading the latest edition of his tourist publication when Josh entered the room. "Hi, son," he said. "Your Mr. Browning called. I've accepted his invitation to photograph some turtle nests tomorrow afternoon on Kauai. You want to come along?"

"Sure!" Josh exclaimed, then asked, "Will it be just you, Tank, and me?"

"If you mean, are the girls coming, too? the answer is no. I asked them, but they said they're going to tour a plant that makes jewelry out of precious coral."

Josh could barely suppress a happy grin. "I'll call Tank and tell him."

"You boys will have tomorrow morning here in

Honolulu," Mr. Ladd added. "We'll fly out at one o'clock."

"Good!" Josh replied, heading for the kitchen phone. "That'll give Tank and me time to make another attempt to get Mr. Catlett to change his mind about Alaska."

"I wouldn't count on that," Mr. Ladd warned.

Josh sighed. *We've got to try*, he thought. *And tomorrow may be our last chance to catch those poachers.*

Chapter Eight

MYSTERY OF THE SEA TURTLES

The next morning after breakfast, Josh was walking down the outside stairs when Kapali drove up with Alicia.

She leaned out of the open car window. "Hi, Josh. You and Tank want to go with Tiffany and me to see how jewelry is made out of coral?"

"No, thanks." Josh kept walking toward the Catletts'.

Alicia slid out of the car to block Josh's way. "The plant doesn't open for a couple of hours. We've got time to all go swimming together at the beach."

"Sorry," Josh replied abruptly, stepping around the girl.

"How about jet skiing instead? Tiffany tells me you guys are pretty good on them."

"We do okay, I guess." Josh knocked on Tank's door.

"Then you could teach . . . " She broke off as Tank opened the door, then said, "Hi, Tank. I just asked Josh if you two would like to teach me how to ride a jet ski. Do you want . . . ?"

"I told her we couldn't," Josh interrupted, kicking off his sandals.

"That's right," Tank agreed, opening the door for Josh to enter. "See you later, Alicia."

Josh went into the apartment and Tank closed the door, leaving the girl standing uncertainly outside. Josh felt a twinge of conscience, but ignored it.

Tank led the way across the white carpet to flop heavily on the flowered couch. "I'll sure be glad when she's gone back to Alaska."

Josh dropped beside his friend. "Yes, but I also feel guilty about the way we treat her."

"She's a pest! How can you feel guilty?"

With a sigh, Josh explained. "She makes me so angry, but then I think what I would feel like if my mom died and I had no sisters or brothers. So I cool down."

"Not me. Just three more days, and she's gone."

"And just three days until your dad may be making plans to move you to Alaska."

"Yeah! Maybe with Alicia as a neighbor." Tank shuddered at the thought. "And with you back here . . . "

"Stop it," Josh interrupted gently but firmly. "We've still got a chance to get our mothers and sisters to try talking your dad out of moving."

"Won't do any good to talk to your sister," Tank replied sourly. "Tiffany obviously likes Alicia—even defends her when she does dumb things. And I've already struck out with Mom and Marsha."

Josh spoke more cheerfully than he felt. "Maybe if we go together ... "

"Can't right now. They're helping decorate the church fellowship hall for some kind of a ladies' event."

"Well, my mother is home. Let's go talk to her now."

Tank squirmed uncomfortably. "Uh ... she'd take one look at how discouraged I am and turn us down. But maybe if you put on a happy face and talked to her ... "

Josh grinned at his friend. "I'll give it a whirl."

***

Reentering his apartment, Josh was glad to see that Tiffany's bedroom door was closed. He could hear the girls speaking softly above some recorded music. Josh was grateful to avoid them. He approached his mother where she was vacuuming the master bedroom.

"Mom," he began over the noisy vacuum cleaner, "Tank and I need you to talk to Mr. Catlett. Please try to get him to stay here so Tank doesn't have to move away."

Mrs. Ladd switched off the vacuum cleaner and turned to face her son. "We have already discussed that, dear. Your father and I agree that we must not interfere in the Catletts' decision. Now, would you run down to the little store and get a head of lettuce? I forgot to get some."

"Aw, Mom! Can't you at least try?"

"You'll find some money in my purse," she said, indicating that her decision was final.

***

Josh felt grumpy and discouraged when he started back from the store. But he was alert enough to notice a sudden movement in the thick oleanders beside the cul-de-sac fence. *Kong!* he thought, stopping and trying to see better.

At the same time, Josh saw Alicia walking down toward the place where Kong waited. Josh glanced around, but Tiffany wasn't in sight. Josh watched Alicia pass Roger where he was fixing a skateboard by the other apartment building. Josh wanted to call a warning to Alicia about Kong. Then he remembered she had led him about by his hair. She could take care of herself.

Josh didn't consider himself a coward, but he also didn't see any sense in walking past Kong alone and taking a chance on getting hurt. Josh turned back, planning to circle around the apartments and come in on the other street.

He had taken only a few steps when Alicia screamed. Josh whirled around to see her standing before Kong.

"No!" she cried. "Leave me alone!"

Josh couldn't see what the bully was doing that threatened Alicia, but she didn't run. She just stood there, screeching. "Let go of me! Let go . . . !"

Josh started running toward her, but Roger was faster. He leaped up, dropped the skateboard, and dashed toward Alicia and Kong.

"You heard her, Kong!" Roger cried angrily. He stopped in front of the big bully and went into a karate stance. "I don't want to hurt you, Kong," Roger warned, "so let go of her!"

"Let go? Kong not . . . "

Alicia interrupted, seeming to struggle to pull her arm back from the bully's hand. "You'd better listen to Roger! He's studied karate, and you don't stand a chance against him now!"

Josh arrived, panting, just as Kong shook his head in confusion at Alicia and Roger.

"You whan* pupule wahine!" Kong said. "And Roger, you planty* pupule, too, yeah?"

"Last chance!" Roger yelled in a high, thin voice.

Kong shrugged and then mumbled, "Kong t'ink big coconuts fall on both you heads. Knock all sense out, yeah?" Slowly, he backed into the oleanders and out of sight.

"Oh, Roger!" Alicia exclaimed, turning to him with shiny eyes. "Thank you! Thank you very much."

Roger's natural shyness around girls immediately returned. He broke his stance and lowered his eyes. "It was nothing."

"Oh, but it was!" the girl replied, turning to Josh. "Wasn't that the bravest thing you ever saw, Josh?"

Josh didn't reply for a moment as he quickly sorted out his thoughts. Then he understood. *Kong didn't touch her. She just pretended, and Roger had to do something.* "Yes," Josh said at last. "Roger, that was something!"

Josh smiled to himself and hurriedly delivered the lettuce to his mother. Then he walked onto the lanai. Josh had never seen Roger talking to a girl alone, but he and Alicia were walking along the cul-de-sac together.

Josh grudgingly admitted to himself, *I've got to give her credit in spite of the dumb things she does.*

The phone rang, so Josh hurried inside to answer it. Tank's voice was sad. "Mom and Marsha came home, so I asked them. But neither will side with me. There goes my last chance."

Josh tried to keep his own terrible sadness from showing in his voice. "Same with my mom. But I'll be right down, and we can talk about it."

The boys sat on the Catletts' lanai and moodily considered their situation. "Unless Dad turns the job down," Tank said in his slow manner of speaking, "I guess I'm moving to Alaska."

Josh didn't answer, knowing from the sick feeling in his stomach that Tank was right. Reluctantly, Josh also admitted to himself that Mr. Catlett was right about promotions in a corporation. A person has to go where the company wants, or that person's career comes to a grinding halt.

Tank added, "That means I'll be in Anchorage where the only person I know is that tomboy pest, Alicia."

Josh started to say that maybe she wasn't so bad, and to tell how she had helped Roger redeem his self-respect. But Josh decided now wasn't the time.

Mrs. Ladd stuck her head over the lanai railing and called down, "Josh, your father is on the phone. He's on his way home to pick you and Tank up for the ride to the airport. You boys had better be ready."

"Okay, Mom," Josh called up. Then he looked thoughtfully at Tank. "This may be the last adventure you and I ever have together. Wouldn't it be great to capture those poachers?"

Tank tried to smile in spite of his misery. "Yeah! One last great adventure! Without the girls along, we might have a chance, huh?"

"Let's hope so," Josh replied cheerfully. "Let's get ready. My dad will be here soon."

***

The biologist and the enforcement officer, both in casual clothes, met their airplane when it landed at Lihue. After Mr. Ladd was introduced to the other two men, they all climbed into the department's unmarked four-wheel-drive vehicle.

"First," Mr. Browning said, "I'll show you the nesting area so you can get your photographs. Then we'll scout around and look for any signs of the poachers."

Mr. Ladd replied, "I really appreciate this opportunity to help publicize the plight of sea turtles, Mr. Browning. Maybe it'll help catch the poachers."

"I hope so, and please call me Gary," the biologist answered, turning his vehicle north on Highway 56.

"Okay, and I'm John," Mr. Ladd said. "I've done a little research on sea turtles, but I'd like your personal observations and comments for my story."

"Well, it's hard to know where to start talking about

harmless creatures that have been swimming the world's oceans for countless ages. Sea turtles are still a big mystery."

Both Josh and Tank leaned forward. "Mystery?" they asked together.

"Yes. You've probably seen films of turtles hatching in the sand and making a desperate run for the water." When both boys nodded, Mr. Browning continued. "But where do they go from there?"

Josh asked, "What do you mean?"

The biologist explained. "Nobody knows where baby sea turtles go as hatchlings. They enter the water and swim out of sight. I personally have never seen an eight-inch sea turtle. They're probably pelagic."

Mr. Ladd explained to the boys that "pelagic means 'that which pertains to the sea or ocean,' like turtles that live near the ocean's surface."

"Very good," Mr. Browning said approvingly. "But you'd be surprised how many people in Hawaii who work around the ocean think that pelagic means 'free swimming.' Anyway, the turtles grow up and return to land. One that's only twenty-eight inches is a teenager. By the time a turtle is thirty-four inches long, it'll weigh around two hundred pounds."

"How big do they get?" Tank wanted to know.

"I've seen them at four hundred pounds. They're sexually mature at thirty-four or thirty-five inches. They can triple their weight in going from thirty to thirty-five inches."

"You mean," Josh questioned, "they'll weigh three times more than they did when they were just five inches shorter?"

"Yes, exactly. When they're mature, the females come ashore when it's calm, usually in July, but sometimes as late as September. They lay their eggs on isolated beaches of both the north and south shores of this island. It takes eggs forty-eight to sixty days to hatch, depending on the temperature. Turtles are cold-blooded reptiles, you know."

The discussion continued until they turned off the highway onto a side road. As they bounced along the rutted road that cut through a sugarcane field, the biologist told about some autopsies he had performed on dead turtles. Some had died from ingesting plastic, which Mr. Browning thought the turtles had swallowed because they mistook it for jellyfish, a favorite food. Then the enforcement officer told stories of how he had apprehended poachers.

The rough road continued until they came to the edge of the sugarcane field. Mr. Browning stopped in an uninhabited area where Josh could see the ocean in the distance.

"We walk from here," the biologist announced.

He and Mr. Kimura led the way toward some ironwood trees. The others followed in single file with Josh at the rear. Except for a horse on a distant hillside overlooking the ocean, there was no sign of any houses or humans.

Near the ironwood trees, footing became tricky because of the slippery needles littering the ground. Josh alternated watching his step, glancing around in hopes of seeing the poachers, and trying not to think about Tank moving to Alaska.

When the ironwood trees were behind them, Mr. Browning continued his explanation. "Sea turtles become resident. They won't even swim to the other side of the island. We know from tagging that ninety-seven percent return to where they were hatched."

Josh whispered to Tank, "I'd sure like to get a chance to catch those poachers, so let's keep a sharp lookout in case they're in the area."

Tank nodded.

Their guides led them down into a small gully that twisted seaward and opened onto the beach.

Mr. Browning switched from turtles to explaining the plants around them. "That's beach naupaka*, and over there are some morning glory vines. To your right are some false almond trees. Their leaves turn red before falling."

Mr. Browning stopped and turned back to speak in a low tone that was barely audible above the sound of the surf. "We don't want to disturb the turtles, so let's be silent from now on."

Only the crunch of their tennis shoes on sand was heard as they rounded a curve to where the ocean spread majestically before them.

Suddenly, Mr. Kimura stopped and held up his hand. As everyone halted, Josh saw a man bending over a turtle.

"Hey there!" the enforcement officer shouted. "What are you doing?"

The stocky haole poacher leaped to his feet. He held a long knife above the turtle, which had been turned on its back. Its legs moved helplessly, scratching the air.

"That's the same man we saw before!" Josh exclaimed.

The poacher whirled around and ran barefooted down the beach, slanting inland toward the ironwood trees.

"Stop!" Mr. Kimura commanded, breaking into a run after the poacher, but the man kept running. Mr. Browning dashed after them.

"You boys wait here," Mr. Ladd said and chased the other three men.

Josh and Tank stood uncertainly as the fugitive and his pursuers quickly disappeared inland beyond a small hill.

Tank muttered, "Now we're not going to get to help catch those poachers. That's not fair."

"At least we can help that turtle. Let's go. . . ." Josh froze. "Someone is coming!"

Both boys crouched down just as another man stepped into view. Josh recognized him as the second poacher.

The man called, "Pete, what's all the shouting about?" He stopped suddenly and looked around suspiciously. "Pete, where are you?" He glanced around and saw the boys. "Hey! What are you kids . . . ?" He broke off his angry cry when his companion shouted in the distance.

Instantly, the brown-skinned poacher spun about and started running back the way he had come.

"Let's get him!" Josh called, racing after the man.

Chapter Nine

A LONG, HARD CHASE

As Josh chased after the fleeing poacher, Tank called, "We'd better wait for your dad and the others."

"No!" Josh raised his voice but kept running. "If we do that, this guy will get away! Come on!"

Josh heard the sound of Tank's tennis shoes as he sprinted to catch up. Josh grinned. *Good ol' Tank! He always comes through. I just hope this isn't the last time!*

The poacher was a strong runner, Josh realized. The man pulled away from the boys until he started up a small hill where long African grass grew in the lonely, desolate area. There Josh and Tank gained on him.

Tank, now panting alongside Josh, said, "I think he's tiring, or we're in better shape than he is. But what are we going to do if we catch him?"

"Maybe we'll just stay close enough to see where he goes. Then Mr. Kimura can arrest him after they catch the other poacher."

The boys ran in silence for a minute, breathing hard.

When they reached the top of the hill, they saw the fleeing man jogging toward a line of ironwood trees.

"You know, there's something strange about all this," Josh panted. "Why should this guy run from a couple of kids?"

"Because he doesn't want to be caught, that's why."

"I think it's a lot more than poaching turtles."

Tank ran a few steps before replying. "You mean, they could be dangerous criminals or something like that?"

"Could be. I don't think they'd run like this if they were just poaching turtles."

Tank slowed his pace slightly. "Uh ... maybe we should wait for your dad and the other two men."

"No, let's keep going and see where this guy is headed. He doesn't have a gun or anything, so he can't hurt us if we stay out of his reach."

The boys neared the line of ironwood trees, which grew thick and close to the ground. The trade winds hissed through their long needles.

The poacher was no longer in sight. Both boys pulled up, breathing hard, and looked around anxiously.

"Hey!" Tank exclaimed, shading his eyes against the sun's glare. "Where did he go?"

"Maybe he's running on the other side of those trees, but they're too thick to see through."

"Yeah, or maybe he's hiding there, waiting to grab us."

"Let's find out," Josh suggested, circling wide around the last tree. His blue eyes probed ahead, but there was still no sign of the poacher.

Tank whispered, "He couldn't just disappear ... "

"Hold it, boys!" The poacher's voice interrupted from behind them. "Don't turn around! Stand still! Get your hands up!"

Josh didn't remember the man having a weapon, but he decided not to take chances. He slowly raised his hands. Tank did the same.

The poacher's voice came again from the denseness of the ironwood trees. "Who are you? What do you want?"

When neither boy replied, the man yelled, "Answer me!"

Josh tried to sound positive. "We're with two men from the Department of Land and Natural Resources. They catch poachers like you. They've already arrested your friend, and they'll come after you any second now."

"Arrested?" The poacher's startled exclamation was followed by his voice sounding fainter. "So that's why he yelled ... "

Josh didn't hear the rest, for he guessed the poacher had turned to look back. Josh stole a glance over his shoulder. He urgently whispered to Tank, "I just got a quick look at him. His hands are empty."

"You sure?" Tank whispered back.

"Yes. He's bluffing. Let's turn and rush him. On the count of three. One ... "

"No, let's just run away!"

"Two ...." Josh continued as though he hadn't heard.

Tank groaned and whirled around when Josh did. Then both stopped abruptly.

The poacher had reached down and snatched up a fallen limb. He swung it viciously. "Fooled you, didn't I?"

"Now, Tank!" Josh whispered. "Let's run!" He spun around, facing inland toward some gently rolling green hills.

"I'm already gone," Tank answered, sprinting away.

"Stop, you dumb kids!" the poacher shouted from behind them. "You can't get away! When I catch you ... "

Josh didn't hear the rest. "Faster, Tank!" Josh urged. "Faster!"

The boys raced into unfamiliar territory and over ancient, uneven lava flows that had only partly been covered by grass and shrubs.

"Careful!" Josh warned, feeling the sharp lava slice into the soles of his tennis shoes. "This footing is pretty tricky! If we fall, we'll really cut ourselves."

Josh desperately hoped his father and the other two men would return with the haole poacher as a prisoner, but there was no sign of them. Josh shifted his frantic gaze to search for a house or even a road that might offer some hope of help. There was none.

Josh struggled to keep going without falling. He ignored a stitch developing in his side and the searing sensation in his tortured lungs.

I've got to rest soon, Josh thought. He risked glancing over his shoulder. "The poacher is falling behind," he gleefully reported to Tank.

"He can't fall too far back to suit me."

Josh's eyes probed ahead. "We'd better circle back or

we'll get lost, and Dad may never find us."

"We can't do that! That guy will cut us off."

"We're coming to a little hill. When we get over the top and out of sight, swing to the left and head for the ocean. If he doesn't see us, we can work our way back toward where we left Dad and the others."

Fighting a desperate need to rest, Josh topped the hill and ran just far enough down it to where their pursuer couldn't see them. "Now, Tank! Turn!"

Both boys suddenly darted sharply to the left.

Josh glanced over his shoulder to see the poacher running straight ahead, down the hill. "We fooled him!" Josh cried in a gleeful stage whisper. "He's still going . . . uh-oh! He's stopping!"

The poacher let out a triumphant yell.

"He's seen us! Here he comes again!"

"But we've got a good lead on him this time! Maybe by the time we get back to where we started . . . "

"No! He's going to cut us off from going back where we started. Head for the ocean. If there's a good beach, maybe we can outrun him and then circle around him."

Almost staggering with exertion, Josh and Tank reached the top of a twenty-foot-high bluff. Looking down at the ocean below them, they saw only a narrow strand of beach with breakers crashing offshore and waves rushing in across the level sand.

Josh commented, "If we can get down there, we can move faster."

The friends found a small cut where rainwater had carved a way down to the beach. In moments, the boys had scrambled down the soft bank and onto the narrow brown strand of beach. They stopped to catch their breath.

Between desperate gasps for air, Tank announced, "There's no sign of him."

Josh anxiously scanned their back trail. "He probably knows this country, and we don't, so we'd better watch out for a surprise. Let's keep moving, but carefully."

Alert, they started walking rapidly along the hard-packed sand. The bluff was to their left; the ocean to their right. Seashells were everywhere, indicating that few people came here to carry them away.

When Tank could breathe almost normally again, he glanced up at the bluff. "Still no sign of him."

Josh didn't reply because his eyes were searching ahead to where the bluff turned slightly inland, obscuring a view of the beach. Josh pointed. "I don't like the looks of that. He could be waiting for us around that bend."

"Yeah, we'd run right into his arms."

The friends automatically slowed and moved closer to the ocean, hoping to see the poacher first if he was planning to ambush them. The waves began rushing in and whirling over their tennis shoes and calves.

"Tide's coming in," Tank observed nervously. "We're soon going to have to get off this beach."

Josh nodded but didn't answer as he eased around the curved bluff. He wondered if his father and the other two men had caught the first poacher. Josh hoped that they had and that now they were looking for them. If not . . . . Josh shook off the terrible thought.

"Almost there," he said softly. "Another few steps and we can see . . . "

He left his sentence unfinished at what he saw before them. There was no sign of the poacher, but there was something almost as terrifying. The high bluff they had been following suddenly veered to the right and ran directly into the sea, totally blocking their way.

"We're trapped!" Tank whispered in anguish. "We can't go back, and if we stay here, we'll drown when the tide comes in!"

Josh swept his gaze over the obstruction, hoping for a way out. But it was obvious the walls were sheer and too steep to climb. Except for some ancient volcanic slabs leaning at sharp angles against the bluff, there was no way to climb out.

Tank moaned, "Now what?"

Josh pointed to where the sea rushed across the narrow strip of sand toward the base of the bluff. The water lapped tentatively at the slabs, then retreated to try again. "We can climb up those," Josh declared.

"No way!" Tank protested. "Volcanic rock is so sharp, it'll cut our hands to pieces."

"It looks to me as if the waves have smoothed the rocks enough that it won't be so bad. Anyway, we can't stay here with the tide coming in so fast, and we certainly can't risk going back." Josh started toward the columns, his wet tennis shoes making squishing noises.

"Wait!" Tank grabbed Josh's arm. "There he is!"

Both boys stopped dead still, watching their pursuer coming along the beach the way they had run. The poacher smiled without humor and slowly approached. He still held the long stick in his right hand and ominously thumped it against his open left palm.

"Ran into my little trap, huh, boys?" he called. "There's no way out, so just stand where you are."

He advanced menacingly, walking just above the waves that surged onto the sand, gaining speed with every rush.

Josh had looked in every direction but saw no way out. Whitecaps formed on the ocean, showing the seas were rough and probably treacherous. Again, Josh's eyes skimmed the length of the bluff to where it plunged into the surging tide. *Can't risk swimming in that*, Josh thought. *There's nothing! Not a thing ... unless ... wait!*

"Come on, Tank!" Josh urged, forcing his tired legs to run toward the volcanic columns.

"What are you doing?"

"I see an old log that's been jammed lengthwise between those volcanic slabs. See it?"

"Yes, but ... "

"Maybe we can climb it like a tree trunk," Josh broke in. "It's the only chance we've got!" Josh raced toward the slabs.

Offshore, a wave crashed ominously. The subsequent

rush of foamy blue-green water almost knocked Josh off his feet. He staggered as the wave retreated, sucking sand from under his shoes.

Finally, Josh reached the water-logged trunk lying against the rocky columns. With a sigh of relief, he saw that some branches still remained, providing a ladder of irregular steps. "It's okay, Tank!" he cried, and he began climbing.

In a few minutes, he and Tank scampered safely onto the top of the bluff. They peered down at the poacher, who was running toward the volcanic rocks, chased by the incoming tide.

"It'll take him a couple of minutes," Josh gasped between ragged breaths. "Let's rest a bit."

"I'd rather keep running."

"Okay, if you want, but my lungs are on fire and I've got a terrible stitch in my side. I'll take only a few moments to catch my breath."

Josh collapsed against the trunks of two ironwood trees that had fallen from a line of similar trees a few feet inland. The smaller trunk, its limbs long gone, lay at right angles across the other one.

"Right about now," Tank replied, wheezing a little as he sat down against the larger trunk, "I think I'd be safer with Alicia for a friend than you."

Josh grinned. "I'm glad you've still got a sense of humor."

"Who says I'm joking?" he replied, but couldn't suppress a grin.

Josh was too winded to say more, but he peeked over the top of the bluff to check on the poacher. Chased by the incoming tide's fury, he had almost reached the volcanic column where the boys had climbed up.

"We've got a few more seconds," Josh decided, again leaning back against the trunk. His memory leaped back to the many adventures he and Tank had shared. *This may be the last one*, he sadly reminded himself. He and Tank would give their lives for the other, he thought. Now they were probably going to be separated if Tank moved to Alaska. *It won't ever be the same without him*, Josh mused.

Tank's voice broke into Josh's melancholy thoughts. "He's getting too close. I'm ready to run again."

Josh nodded and reached up to grasp the trunk to help himself to his feet. He stopped as the smaller trunk moved under his hand.

"Careful," he warned Tank. "That one is loose."

"Okay." Tank used the lower trunk to pull himself up. "I think I see your dad and the others over that way." He pointed. "Yes, and they've caught the other poacher!"

"Great! Too bad we can't catch this one . . . ." Josh stopped, looking thoughtfully at the crossed tree trunks.

"Come on," Tank urged.

"Just a minute."

Tank hesitated. "What are you thinking?"

"If we could roll this little trunk to the edge of the bluff where that man could see it . . . "

"Yeah!" Tank's eyes lit up with understanding. "We can

tell him to go back or we'll roll the trunk over on him!"

"We can threaten, but we can't do it. If he goes back to the beach, the tide will get him."

"Then let's run!"

Josh hesitated. "Not yet. I think maybe there's another way."

"He's almost to the top, and he's still got that big stick!" Tank warned, taking a quick look down.

"But we've got this tree trunk," Josh countered, his thoughts churning rapidly. "Here, help me move it."

"What?" Tank's voice rose in anguished protest.

"Hurry! I'll explain later." Josh seized one end of the smaller trunk and began easing it across the larger, supporting one.

"Now I know I'd rather have Alicia for a friend," Tank complained, reaching down to help Josh.

"If you don't hurry, that poacher may get us and neither of us will have any friends."

A smile played briefly across Tank's face. "I sure hope you know what you're doing," he said.

"Me, too," Josh answered and quickly explained his plan.

Chapter Ten

DECISION TIME

The boys wrestled the smaller trunk to the edge of the bluff.

Josh instructed, "Let's shove the end out where he can see it clearly."

When that was done, Josh leaned over the top of the bluff and called down to the poacher, who was only about six feet below, "Stop right there!"

"Hey, kid, when I get hold of you ... "

"Careful!" Josh interrupted. "If you make us nervous, my friend and I could give this old tree trunk a little shove, and it would fall right about on top of you."

"Yeah!" Tank added, placing his foot on the log so the end teetered ominously downward. "Don't make us nervous!"

The poacher stopped climbing, his eyes on the end of the trunk. "I've got a friend, too, you know. When he gets here ... "

"He's not coming," Tank broke in cheerfully. "We just

saw him taken prisoner by the . . . what do they call it, Josh?"

"The Division of Aquatic Resources for the Department of Land and Natural Resources."

"Yeah, that," Tank told the poacher. "Your friend is on his way to jail, and those two men who caught him are coming to help us take you to jail, too."

"You're bluffing!" The poacher's voice was gruff, but there was a hint of doubt in it. "I'm coming up!"

"I'm sorry to hear that," Josh answered, reaching down to the teetering trunk. "If you're fortunate, maybe this will just knock you back into the ocean."

"Yeah!" Tank added. "Then you can see how good a swimmer you are in rough water."

The climber swiveled his head to glance down just as a monstrous wave broke offshore. A foaming mass of swirling water rushed inland across the narrow beach. The wave didn't stop until it touched the foot of the man's perch. It sloshed up to his feet. Then, hissing and sucking, as though warning that it would reach higher next time, the water retreated.

Josh's eyes sought previous high-water marks on the face of the bluff. Based on his observation, he didn't think the water would quite reach the poacher. However, Josh was sure the man hadn't noticed that.

"Next time," Josh warned, "it'll be higher. In a little while, it'll reach you. I hope you can hang on real tight when that happens."

"Unless," Tank added cheerfully, "you drop your stick and tell us what we want to know."

The poacher silently considered this as he watched the next tidal surge. This time the wave broke with more force against the volcanic column. It threw a shower of spray that soaked the man's pants to his knees.

He looked up as the water again drained off the narrow beach. "No kids are going to stop me!"

He reached up and gripped the next highest limb on the inclined tree trunk.

"It was your choice, mister," Josh said before turning to Tank. "Let's shove this trunk over and then move the next one in place in case this one misses."

Both boys bent and inched the smaller trunk out a couple of inches to where it tilted ominously at the edge of the bluff.

"Wait! Stop!" The poacher's frantic shout made both boys hesitate and look down at him. He threw his stick into the retreating wave. "Let me out of here, and I'll tell you whatever you want to know."

Josh replied with a shake of his head. "We'll let you climb a little higher, but not all the way out. If we let you do that, you might decide to do something foolish."

"But if I stay here, I'll drown when the tide comes in!" The poacher's voice rose in fear. "Let me up!"

Josh took another glance at previous high-water marks on the face of the bluff. He felt confident that the tide would never reach higher than the man's knees. However, there was a possibility he would slip and be carried out to sea.

Josh whispered, "We'd better let him up."

"Wait!" Tank whispered back, looking over his shoulder. "Here come your dad and the two department men."

Josh stole a peek backward and confirmed that all three were running hard in the boys' direction. Josh got a glimpse of their prisoner in the backseat of the department's vehicle.

Josh turned to again look down at the slender local poacher. "We'll let you up on one condition: tell us what you and your friend have been doing."

With a glance at the surging tide, now almost to his shoes, the poacher cried, "You already know that! We just killed a couple of turtles, that's all."

"I don't think so," Josh assured him.

"Yeah!" Tank added. "Tell us what else you're doing. The next wave might sweep you off that tree."

The incoming tide slid noisily across the narrow beach. It sloshed and gurgled against the bluff, then swirled around the poacher's ankles.

"All right! All right!" he yelled. "I'll tell! We're helping smuggle dope ashore."

Josh and Tank exchanged triumphant grins, then both looked down and asked together, "How?"

"Let me up, and I'll tell you."

"You tell us, and then we'll let you up," Tank replied grimly. "Huh, Josh?"

Josh nodded. "That's right. So talk fast."

Offshore, the next wave broke with an explosion like

thunder and started rolling inland.

"All right! All right! A boat brings in bags of drugs in watertight containers. They drop them over and we take our boat and recover them. Then we pass them on to our contact. Now, let me up, please!"

Josh looked back and saw that his father, the biologist, and the enforcement officer were within a few yards.

"Start up slowly," Josh said, "and while you're doing that, tell us when the next boat is coming in and the name of the person to whom you deliver the drugs."

Moments later, when Josh's father, Mr. Browning, and Mr. Kimura arrived to take charge of the second prisoner, the boys were able to pass on the latest information.

"Well done, boys!" Mr. Kimura said, clapping them on their shoulders. "You've not only stopped some turtle poachers, but you've broken up a drug ring, too!"

Mr. Browning added with a smile, "You two can be proud of this day's work."

***

On the flight back to Honolulu, Mr. Ladd looked across the aisle at Josh and Tank. "You're both very quiet," he commented. "You should be happy for what you've done."

Josh, sitting on the aisle, shrugged. "I guess we're both thinking that this probably was our last adventure together. And it wasn't all that exciting."

"Oh, I thought it was!" Mr. Ladd replied. "Mr. Browning and Mr. Kimura caught one man while I took pictures. You boys captured the other poacher and made him confess to smuggling drugs. Now not only will the sea turtles be safe, but the Marine Patrol will seize the next incoming load of contraband, and the police will grab the island distributor. You boys get credit for all that."

Josh sighed. "Just the same, I was hoping we could have had a lot more exciting adventure if this is going to be our last one."

At the window seat, Tank turned from where he had been moodily staring out at the ocean. "Yeah, we'd like a really big one!"

Mr. Ladd smiled teasingly. "Don't give up hope, boys. From what you've told me about Alicia, there's still time for that."

Josh said somberly, "You're just saying that to cheer us up, Dad."

Mr. Ladd sighed. "I guess I was at that."

Everyone fell silent. Josh's thoughts drifted to the possibility of what tomorrow might bring. Would Tank's father announce his decision about moving to Alaska? The thought of being separated from Tank made Josh's stomach churn. It was still that way when they landed at Honolulu and headed for the parking lot where Mr. Ladd had left his old station wagon.

Nobody spoke until Mr. Ladd steered the vehicle under the carport behind the apartment building. As they were getting out of the station wagon, Alicia's father arrived in a taxi.

After exchanging greetings, he asked Tank, "Has your father announced his decision about Alaska yet?"

"Not yet," Tank answered glumly.

"Cheer up," Mr. Wharton urged, following Mr. Ladd and the two boys up the outside stairs. "If he does, you'll learn to love Alaska just as the rest of us do."

"Not without Josh," Tank replied.

"Maybe you'll live near us, and you'll have Alicia to pal around with," her father said.

Josh heard Tank almost choke as he suppressed a groan.

Everyone stopped at the top of the second-story stairs and removed their shoes.

Mr. Wharton continued, "In the summer, you can mine for gold. Or you can fly with my daughter and me to some of the lodges I own on different lakes. A float plane is the only way to reach them. Or we can switch to a ski plane and land on a real glacier or a hidden lake."

"I don't care," Tank replied even more glumly.

Mr. Ladd unlocked the door and everyone entered the Ladds' apartment.

"Mary? Tiffany?" Mr. Ladd called. "We're home. Trent Wharton is with us."

There was no answer, but a note on the refrigerator explained that Mrs. Ladd and the two girls had walked down to the neighborhood store. They would be back shortly.

"Have a seat, Trent," Mr. Ladd said, entering the kitchen. "I'll get us some refreshments."

"Sounds good, John," Alicia's father replied. He dropped into a rattan chair and stretched his legs out before him. "Boys, while we've got a minute, let me tell you more about Alaska."

Tank shook his head. "Sorry, Mr. Wharton, but I have to get downstairs and see if my dad is home."

"This will take only a minute, Tank," the Alaskan replied, patting the seat of the matching rattan sofa next to him. "Take a load off your feet."

Josh understood how anxious Tank was to know about his father's decision, but Josh also wanted his friend to hear what the visitor had to say. "Sit for a minute, Tank," Josh urged.

"Good idea," Mr. Ladd replied, returning with a tray and four cans of cold soft drinks.

As the boys sat on the sofa, Mr. Wharton accepted a beverage from his host and continued. "In Alaska, you'll meet families that build their own cabins and live off the land. They pick wild berries, and some people grow their own vegetables and put stuff up for the winter. The men hunt or fish. Some kids are home schooled."

Josh confessed, "That's all very interesting. But why do people go to Alaska in the first place? I mean, unless their company transfers them?"

"Lots of reasons," Wharton replied. "Some just want to get away. Some want to write. Some like the challenge. Personally, I like the wide open spaces.

"There are no roads in many places, so we go by float

planes and land on the lakes. All around are majestic mountains, sort of like Switzerland. Some people are climbers
who enjoy tackling the many mountains in Alaska. And, of
course, there's fishing and wild animals."

Josh wanted to say, "That sounds wonderful," but he
didn't want to possibly offend Tank. Instead, Josh asked,
"What's the most exciting thing that ever happened to you,
Mr. Wharton?"

"Well, let's see." He took a sip of his drink before con-
tinuing. "There have been so many." He glanced toward
the door. "I think I hear the ladies coming."

Mrs. Ladd entered, followed by Tiffany and Alicia.

"Hey, Dad," Alicia said, walking barefooted across the
room to stand beside her father's chair. "Since tomorrow
is our last day, is it okay if Kapali drives all of us kids
around the island?"

"Sure, baby," he replied, giving her hand a little
squeeze. "I've been reading John's tourist—uh, visitor—
newspaper and saw several places I think you might like
to see. Like Punchbowl*, Pearl Harbor*, and the memorial
over the battleship Arizona*. These boys will make good
guides . . . "

"I can't go," Tank broke in. He stood up quickly. "And I
have to get downstairs."

"What's the hurry?" Alicia asked as the phone rang.

Tiffany, as usual, raced to answer it, always expecting
that the call was for her.

Alicia continued, "We want to hear about what you

guys did on Kauai today."

"Josh can tell you," Tank replied, heading for the door.

"Wait, Tank," Tiffany said, extending the phone toward him. "It's Marsha. Says it's important."

The boys exchanged anxious glances before Tank took the instrument and said hello to his sister.

Josh studied his friend's face and knew the answer before Tank wordlessly replaced the phone in its cradle.

"Dad just called," he said tonelessly. "He's accepted the transfer to Alaska."

"Great!" Alicia exclaimed.

Tank gave her such a hard look that she seemed to wither. She stood silently as Tank walked out the door without even saying good-bye to anyone.

Josh felt a wave of sickness sweep over him, followed by a terrible sense of loss and loneliness. "Excuse me," he said, leaping up and hurrying down the hall toward his bedroom.

He flopped facedown on his bed and pulled a pillow over his head. *Why?* The question leaped to his mind and burned with a white-hot intensity. *Why? Why? Why?* he asked, pounding his fist into the mattress. *It's not fair! We're best friends. Always have been. Always will be. We belong together, but now . . .*

He broke off his miserable thoughts at a knock on his door.

"It's Mom," said a voice through the door. "May I come in?"

Josh removed the pillow from over his head, ran the back of his hand across his eyes, and sat up. "Okay."

Mrs. Ladd entered the room and sat down on the edge of Josh's bed. "Alicia and her father have gone. Your dad wanted to come to talk to you, but I asked him to let me," she said, taking Josh's hand. "You want to talk about it?"

"There's no use talking," Josh replied dully. "Tank is moving away, and I may never see him again. That hurts, Mom! It hurts something awful—even worse than the last time!"

"I know, but you will see him again. We'll visit Alaska, and Tank's family will probably come here from time to time."

"It won't be the same!" Josh's voice rose and almost cracked with the intensity of his pain.

"You knew this might happen."

"Yes, but I didn't really believe it, Mom! I can't understand why it's happening!"

"There are some things in life that nobody can understand or explain. In times like that, we must put our trust in God and leave things in His hands."

"I don't want to do that, Mom. I want to be with Tank, no matter what!"

"Sometimes we don't get a choice, as in this case."

"I can't accept that, Mom! I just can't!"

They talked a while longer, and then Josh said he would like to be alone. His mother patted his hand and left.

Josh sat on the edge of his bed and stared out the

window. Both his and Tank's worlds had crumbled, and Josh mentally cast about in the ruins, angrily asking why, unwilling to accept the calamity.

He looked up at the Hawaiian sky, at the fluffy white clouds floating on a sea of purest blue.

His mind jumped back to his dog, Chico. For years he, Tank, and Chico had played together. Then Chico grew old and died. Josh had cried for weeks before he could accept the fact that there were some things nobody could change.

Slowly, painfully, Josh worked through his latest grief. Words sifted into his mind: *Not my will* . . . . Josh had never been able to say that before, but now he did. "Not my will," he said softly. "Whatever happens, somehow, someway, I'll deal with it."

Sometimes a person had to accept things on faith that everything would work out. With that thought, a sense of peace began seeping over him, a feeling of acceptance mixed with deep sadness.

He heard the telephone ring down the hallway and thought he should go call Tank. At least they could still talk together. He got up and opened the door just as his sister called to him.

"Tank is on the phone. Says he has to talk to you right away. Don't call him back, he said. Just hurry and come right down."

Josh dashed toward the door, wondering what urgent news Tank had to share.

Chapter Eleven

THE WITCH'S CAULDRON

T ank met Josh at the screen door. "Guess what?"

"What? What?" Josh asked impatiently.

"Mom just called Dad at work, and they're going to let me come back here to visit you next year."

Josh suppressed a sigh of relief and followed his friend across the rug, where both flopped down on the sofa.

"That's great," Josh said, forcing himself to sound cheerful. After all, a visit was better than nothing, although a visit certainly would never compare with being together daily.

He started to ask some questions just as Roger called from outside. Josh and Tank joined him.

"I hear da kine news from Manuel 'bout you fambly gonna move Alaska," Roger said, lapsing into Pidgin English. "Tank, we goin' miss you heah*, 'cause you whan good malihini*."

"Mahalo*," Tank replied. "You're really okay in my book, too."

117

Roger switched to regular English. "Manuel and I talked to our mothers, and they said it's all right to give you a little going-away party. Maybe tomorrow night. Is that okay with you, Tank?"

Josh was touched by this gesture.

He could see that Tank was also moved, although he protested, "Aw, you guys don't have to do that."

"We want to," Roger assured him. "We just need to know if tomorrow night is a good time for you."

"I'll have to check with my parents," Tank replied. "But I'm pretty sure it'll be okay."

"Call me tonight after your dad gets home," Roger urged. "We want to invite every kid in the neighborhood."

"Don't forget Kong," Tank said jokingly.

Roger frowned. "I think maybe we could invite him."

"You're kidding!" Josh exclaimed.

"Yeah!" Tank added. "The idea of that big bully at a party is so wild it cracks me up!"

Roger shook his head. "Both Manuel and I have noticed that he's been sort of different lately. I thought it was because he was scared of my learning karate. But Manuel says it's something else."

"Oh?" Josh was genuinely curious.

Roger shrugged. "Manuel thinks it has something to do with Alicia."

Tank groaned and rolled his eyes upward. "Oh, no!"

Josh was so surprised that he didn't say anything.

Roger continued. "Anyway, whether we ask Kong or

not, we're going to invite Alicia, Tiffany, and Marsha to the party."

Josh stared, scarcely able to believe that Roger was serious. His somber face said he was.

Josh knew that Roger had always been shy around girls. That is, until he had rescued Alicia from Kong—or at least it appeared he had saved her. Josh had no intention of letting Roger know the truth. Let him enjoy his new self-image.

Josh saw that Tank's mouth had dropped open in utter surprise. "Invite girls?" Tank managed to say in a strangled voice. He quickly cleared his throat and added, "I mean, I thought it would be just all us guys who hang around together."

"It can be," Roger admitted.

Josh noticed the hint of disappointment in Roger's voice. "Uh, Tank," Josh began, "maybe you'd like to think about this?"

Tank hesitated briefly before answering. "No, Roger, if you and Manuel want to give me a party, you should invite anybody you want."

As Roger left to tell Manuel, Tank muttered under his breath. Then he turned to Josh and said, "I don't want Alicia there, but what else could I say, Josh?"

"You did the right thing."

"I hope she doesn't ruin the party."

"She'll soon be gone."

"Yeah, but I may be, too."

Noting the sadness in Tank's remark, Josh slapped his friend on the shoulder. "Don't think about that. Instead, let's think about tomorrow. Since it's the last full day she'll be here, Alicia wants us to show her some places on the island that she hasn't seen before."

"Oh, great!" Tank muttered with heavy sarcasm. "Sounds like a fun day!"

* * *

The next morning, Kapali drove up with Alicia. Josh, Tank, and Tiffany slid into the backseat, and they all headed down the cul-de-sac. Alicia turned from where she sat by the driver.

"Tank, isn't it super of Roger and Manuel to give you a party and invite all us girls?"

"Super," Tank said under his breath.

Josh gently poked his elbow into Tank's ribs as a reminder to be nice.

Alicia didn't seem to notice Tank's lack of enthusiasm. She unfolded a map of Oahu on her lap. "I've marked some places I want to see," she said. "Kapali knows where they all are, but I want to follow along and mark the map. That way I can show friends back home where I went in Hawaii. That includes the Witch's Cauldron. I want to see it again."

Alarm bells sounded in Josh's mind. "Oh, no!" he exclaimed, leaning forward in the seat. "Let's stay away from there."

"I'll be careful," Alicia promised. "We'll do that last and then head back for tonight's party."

Josh tried again. "I really don't think . . . "

Alicia interrupted. "Well, I'm going! The rest of you can stay in the car, but I want to get some pictures to show people back home."

She said it with such finality that Josh realized further discussion was useless. Tank and Tiffany seemed to get the same feeling, because they were silent. Josh slouched back in the seat and stared blindly out the window as the car passed various familiar sites.

The warm Hawaiian sun was sailing high in the morning sky when Kapali approached the Witch's Cauldron. They drove past some jet skiers riding their power craft off the beach a short distance from the cauldron.

"Hey, you guys," Alicia said, "that's something we haven't done yet—jet ski."

Josh replied, "There isn't time today."

"We could take time," Alicia declared. "That is, unless you and Tank aren't nearly as good on those things as Tiffany told me you are."

Tank said gruffly, "Josh and I don't have to prove to you that we can handle those pretty well."

"Take my word for it," Tiffany added. "Even I'm impressed with what they can do on jet skis."

Josh flashed his sister a grateful smile.

Alicia was persistent. "All the more reason why you boys should show me. As soon as I snap my pictures, I'll rent a couple of jet skis and judge you for myself."

Tank rolled his eyes up in angry resignation, but Josh said nothing.

Kapali parked within sight of the infamous Witch's Cauldron. Alicia put her map away and took out her camera to look through the viewfinder.

After a moment, she announced, "I have got to get closer."

"No!" Josh exclaimed. "It's not safe!"

"See those girls standing over there by the edge?" Alicia asked, pointing. Two teenagers had ventured onto the volcanic area behind and above the partially submerged cave. Alicia added, "I'll go over by them."

Kapali rarely said much, but he spoke as a cautious adult. "A big wave could suddenly ..."

"Quit worrying, everybody!" Alicia broke in, sliding out of the car. She hurried away with her camera.

Josh turned to Tiffany. "Why didn't you say something? She might have listened to you."

"She wouldn't a little while ago. Besides, she'll only be a minute."

Tank muttered disapprovingly, "Pupule wahine."

Josh shook his head in resignation. In spite of his concern, he got out of the car to see the cauldron better. Tank and Tiffany joined him.

From a slightly higher vantage point, Josh could see Alicia nearing the two teenage girls. They were running with delighted shrieks from a wave that had been thrown high in the air and forward above the cave. The water landed with a crash on the bare volcanic rock, splattering the giggling girls. When the wave started draining back into the basin, the laughing girls chased after it until they came to where the cave reappeared from the boiling, foaming cauldron.

Josh turned to Tank. "They're taking too big a risk getting that close."

"Yeah. They're probably Mainland malihinis who don't know how dangerous it is."

Tiffany added, "I think Alicia is getting too close."

Josh cupped his hands to his mouth and called. "Alicia, don't go any closer! A big wave could . . . "

Alicia turned around and gave Josh an annoyed look. "Quit worrying!" she yelled. "If you're afraid, wait in the car."

Josh was tempted to turn back in disgust, but he glanced beyond Alicia and saw that the two teenagers were looking at him with sudden interest.

He cupped his hands again and called to them. "You're risking your lives! Get away before . . . !"

Tank's frantic call from behind stopped him. "Josh!" There was terror in his voice. "Look! Look!"

Swiveling to his left, Josh glanced seaward and sucked in his breath. An unusually large wave had just poured over the hidden reef and was rushing toward shore. The water was immediately forced into the narrow volcanic channel leading to the turbulent, foamy bowl with the cave at the end.

Frightened for the girls, Josh pivoted back to his right. Alicia, who had now joined the two teenagers, lifted the camera to her eyes, apparently focusing on the wave surging toward her.

Josh motioned wildly with his hands. "Run!" he shouted, fear giving authority to his voice. "Alicia! Girls! Run! Run!"

The two teenagers obeyed, automatically scrambling away from the menace bearing down on them like an avenging flood. Alicia held her ground, her forefinger moving quickly as she snapped pictures.

"Alicia!" Josh's voice was a hoarse cry of alarm.

Alicia lowered the camera, then recoiled in horror. Obviously, the monstrous wave now towering above her was a thousand times bigger and more menacing than what she had seen in the tiny viewfinder. She dropped the camera and raced after the other two girls.

Josh started sprinting toward them, although he knew he was too far away to help. He saw the wave crash down and explode into the cave. A sliver of the opening showed for a second before the air inside was forced out with a hollow roar. The cave vanished underwater as the last part of the monster wave rose above the barren volcanic land where the three girls were trying to outrun the danger.

But it was too late. As the suspended wave fell, it knocked one teenager and Alicia off their feet.

"Oh, Lord, no!" Josh cried.

The wave retreated rapidly, like a giant octopus pulling

victims back to its lair. Josh heard himself shouting, but he had no knowledge of what he was saying, terror numbing his mind.

The other girl, scratching frantically for a fingerhold on the barren rock, lost her grip. She cartwheeled off balance and rolled sideways toward the beach. The water streamed away, leaving her soaked and bruised but safe. Her companion darted to safety on the nearby sand.

The top of the cave suddenly reappeared from under the water. For a moment, the wide gash of the cave's entrance reminded Josh of a gigantic mouth grinning diabolically. Alicia screamed, still trying to get a grip on the wet, slippery bank of the basin, but the retreating water pulled her down. For a moment, she seemed to have checked her slide. Then the force of the water broke her grip, and she plummeted feet first into the Witch's Cauldron.

Josh reached the bank just as Alicia disappeared under the water. The boy's natural inclination was to jump in and save her, but he realized that that would be foolish and futile. If he did it, there would be two people to save—or drown.

For an instant, Josh stood uncertainly, his mind racing with futile possibilities.

Alicia's head popped up in the middle of the seething mass. Her pixie haircut was barely visible as the powerful undercurrent started sucking her toward the open sea.

Josh spun around to see Tank, Kapali, and Tiffany running toward the terrible scene. "Get help!" Josh yelled, his throat torn by the urgency of his cry. "Find a lifeguard. Call the Coast Guard or the fire department. Tank, see if you can find a rope. Hurry! Hurry!"

Without waiting for an answer, Josh turned back toward the Witch's Cauldron. It took him a second to locate Alicia's bobbing head among the furious swirls of white water.

Then he saw her. She faced him, her eyes wide with fright. Her arms stroked vigorously but uselessly. The tide was too strong for her to swim free.

"Hang on!" Josh yelled, hoping she could hear him above the wild water. "We'll get you out."

If she heard, Alicia gave no sign. She kept trying to paddle, but only her arms and shoulders showed. Josh guessed that the undertow was dragging her feet down.

Josh ran along the basin's edge, shouting encouragement and trying to keep from falling in.

Tank appeared beside Josh. "Where is she?"

Josh pointed. "There!"

"That's better than being in that cave." Without waiting for Josh to reply, Tank added, "Kapali ran down the beach to see if any of those swimmers have a rope. Tiffany is looking for a telephone."

Josh suddenly gripped his friend's arm. "Look! Alicia is slowing up! The tide is about to turn! Maybe now she can swim out!" He cupped his hands to call encouragement, but stopped when Tank grabbed his arm.

"Look!" Tank cried, his voice high with fear. "She's

going to be carried back to where she started!"

"Worse than that!" Josh exclaimed. "She'll be swept into the cave and drowned!" He again cupped his hands and shouted, "Swim, Alicia! Swim this way! Swim hard!"

She tried, but it was useless. The incoming wave picked her up like a leaf and violently propelled her toward the cave's yawning mouth. An instant later, she was swept into it. Everything disappeared under tons of furious white water.

Chapter Twelve

URGENT EFFORTS

Josh watched in terror as the violent waters buried the entire cave. He wondered if Alicia could hold her breath until the turbulent tide changed directions. In a few seconds that seemed forever, the water started draining back into the basin.

While Josh watched in helpless anxiety, the top of the cave appeared—then the opening. But not Alicia.

Tank cried, "She's trapped inside!"

Josh didn't answer. He peered hopefully at the water still flowing out of the cave. He recalled the horror stories he had heard about people getting swept into island caverns where they drowned.

"Come on, Alicia! Come on!" he whispered hoarsely, hoping to see her disgorged from her trap. But there was still no sign of her.

Tank exclaimed angrily, "She makes me so mad! She wouldn't listen! Now she's going to die in there!"

Josh had also been angry with Alicia, and now he was

furious with her because her own foolhardiness had put her in terrible danger. This also put Josh and Tank in a fearful position, because now they faced an awful choice: to stand by helplessly or to try saving her by risking their own lives.

Suddenly, all Josh's resentment toward the girl vanished. He didn't know how, but he knew that something had to be done—and fast.

He tore his eyes away from the cave and the foaming white froth of the Witch's Cauldron. "We've got to save her!" he cried to Tank. "Look around! See if you can spot something we can use until help comes!"

"Nothing can go in that cave!" Tank declared, spinning around to glance in all directions. "Even if she gets carried out again, what can we do?"

It was a terrible question for which Josh had no answer. He looked around frantically, seeing people from the beach running toward the cauldron. He spotted his sister leaning into a car window and talking to someone.

"Tiffany has found someone with a car phone!" Josh cried.

"Yeah! And here comes Kapali with a rope. But that won't do any good!"

"It might if Alicia gets flushed out of there!"

"*If,*" Tank repeated softly.

Josh didn't answer, but waved and shouted, urging Kapali to greater speed. He was already running flat out, trailed by a group of people. The jet skiers had abandoned their crafts at the beach and joined the rush toward the center of excitement.

The boys turned back to face the basin. Josh gulped. "Alicia!" He pointed. "She's out!"

She bobbed in front of the cave, her arms lifting in a vain effort to swim free of the mad waters as they swirled in the cauldron's turbulence.

Kapali arrived, puffing hard, holding on to a coil of light yellow nylon rope. "It's only fifty feet," he explained. "Not long enough to be much good, but if . . . where is she?"

Josh pointed. "There, in the middle of that foam. It's pretty far, but maybe we can throw it close enough that she can grab it." He glanced at the rope. "You're bigger and stronger, Kapali. You throw it."

The man nodded and shook out the end, then stopped. "The end is too light," Kapali explained. "It won't carry far without some weight. We need to tie something on that will float instead of sinking."

Josh and Tank spun about, scanning the crowd that had gathered around to watch the drama. Most of them were teenagers, but there was one young couple also standing there. The woman was holding a small Styrofoam ice chest, while the man held a child wearing a life jacket with brightly colored Hawaiian flowers.

"Please, mister," Tank pleaded, running up to the father. "Let me borrow her jacket."

With a quick nod of understanding, the man set his daughter down, but Josh stopped him. "That's not heavy enough." He turned toward the woman and touched the ice chest. "May we use this?"

The woman handed it over. "It's empty."

"Great! Thanks!" Josh took the chest and handed it to Kapali.

Kapali quickly checked to see that the top was securely in place. Then he tied the rope through the handle and started swinging the chest over his head by the short end of the rope.

"Hurry!" Josh urged. "A wave is coming in!"

Josh watched in fascinated horror as Alicia's course changed. The incoming surge again sent her shooting help-lessly toward the cave's gaping mouth.

The whirling rope suddenly left Kapali's hands, send-ing the ice chest sailing over the basin, trailing the light yel-low rope. The chest reached the top of its trajectory, hung for a moment in the air, then fell into the water.

The chest landed a few feet short of Alicia's grasping hands. "I'll try again!" Kapali cried, frantically pulling the rope back. "I hope this chest doesn't break from hitting the water." He reached for the chest just as the crowd gasped loudly.

Alicia again disappeared into the cave, and water cov-ered the opening.

Josh looked at Tank's stricken face and said hopefully, "We'll get her the next time."

"I hope there is a next time," Tank replied quietly.

Kapali gave them some encouragement. "I remember

hearing about this cave from another rescue long ago. The person gets pinned against the back wall by the force of the water. But an air pocket forms at the top of the cave, so if the person can hold his breath until the water drains out, there's air to breath even if he can't get out."

Josh nodded, then silently joined the crowd in waiting to see if the girl would reappear. When she didn't, he asked fearfully, "Do they always come out?"

Kapali slowly shook his head. "No." There was great sadness in the single word.

A spontaneous cheer from the crowd turned Josh's attention from Kapali to the basin. Alicia was again borne out of the deadly prison into the foaming water.

"The rope!" Josh cried, turning to Kapali, who had already anticipated the possibility and was ready. "Throw it again!"

The little ice chest at the end of the rope whirled over Kapali's head for a few seconds, then again sailed out over the bubbling water. The chest fell about three feet in front of the bobbing girl.

"Pretty close! Good!" Tank exclaimed. He cupped his hands and yelled, "Swim for it, Alicia! Swim hard!"

The crowd caught the name and joined in shouting their encouragement. "Swim, Alicia! Swim for it!"

Josh felt himself grow tense as he willed her by the power of his mind and body to make the few quick strokes necessary to catch up to the floating chest. Then the truth hit him.

"She's tiring! She can barely lift her arms!"

"Yes," Tank answered, "but if she can just take a couple more strokes . . . "

The crowd's groan of disappointment interrupted him. An erratic eddy suddenly seized the chest and whirled it away, completely out of reach. At the same moment, another incoming wave caught Alicia and again bore her helplessly toward the cave.

The crowd shrieked in terror and shouted for Kapali to hurry. He frantically pulled the rope in, his brown hands blurring as he recovered the nylon. It fell in glistening wet coils at his feet.

Josh heard his name being called and turned to see his sister dash up, out of breath from desperate running. "A man let me use his car phone," she panted. "The fire department's rescue squad is on its way." When her brother nodded, Tiffany glanced over the basin, let out a frightened sob, and clamped both hands over her mouth. "Is it too late?"

"She's in the cave," Josh explained. "Been carried in there twice." He motioned toward Kapali, who stood with the rope ready to throw again. "But she's tiring so much, she might not even be able to hang on now, even if she reaches the rope."

"Then we've got to do something else!" Tiffany cried.

"But what?" Josh hopefully glanced out to sea, but there wasn't a boat in sight. He skimmed the beach, now empty of people. Only a few jet skis rested on the sand.

Josh started to turn back to join the waiting crowd when his eyes flashed back on the beach. "Tank!" he shouted, hope sending his voice shooting up. "Come with me!" He grabbed his friend's arm and started dashing toward the beach.

"Where are we going?" Tank wanted to know.

"I think I see the only way to save Alicia."

"There's nothing over in that direction!"

"Save your breath, Tank! You'll need it!"

Josh ran with all possible speed, his eyes sweeping the abandoned jet skis. *It'll take both Tank and me*, he told himself, trying to think ahead. *I thought I saw one with . . . yes! I did. There it is!*

Breathing heavily, Josh raced to the jet ski that he had remembered. *Please, Lord, let it start!*

Tank asked through ragged gasps for air, "What are you doing?"

"The guy who drove this jet ski was towing somebody on that big inner tube. See?" Josh motioned briefly toward the black tube that had once been in a tractor tire, but his eyes were on the jet ski. With a silent prayer, he pushed the unit into the water, dragging the tube behind. He reached down and pulled the starter.

"Yes!" Josh yelled triumphantly as the motor roared to life. "Tank, there's only one way to reach Alicia, and that's with this thing." He patted the console over the powerful motor. "You jump on that inner tube. I'll ride straight up to her, and you pull her onto the tube and hang on!"

Tank shook his head dubiously and yelled to be heard above the engine. "That'll never work! What if the motor dies? Without power, we'll all . . . "

"I know! I know! But can you think of anything else?"

Tank made a sobbing, moaning sound and shook his head.

Josh said, "You don't have to go . . . "

Tank broke in. "Yes, I do. It'll take both of us. Let's go!" He bent and quickly threw himself facedown across the inner tube, then gripped the rope that had been wrapped around to serve as a hand grip.

With a quick, silent prayer, Josh opened the throttle and headed for the opening to the channel. He tried to avoid thinking of all the terrible things that could happen. Instead, he concentrated on his goal.

By the time he slackened speed to turn toward the cave, he saw another set of waves building offshore behind them. "Hang on, Tank!" Josh shouted. "Here we go!"

He again opened the throttle. Aided by the incoming waves, he sped down the channel toward the ominous Witch's Cauldron. It looked more dangerous than ever, and Josh's mouth went dry with fear.

He was still trying to adjust to this unfamiliar jet ski, so he didn't dare look up at the crowd. Instead, he kept his eyes probing ahead, hoping against hope to see Alicia's head and shoulders.

Got to see her in time, he warned himself. *Must not run her down. But where is she?*

There was no sign of Alicia as the jet ski hurtled out of the channel and into the basin's bubbling white mass of water. Fighting a sense of despair, Josh stood up, trying to gain height so he could see better.

She must still be in the cave, he realized, and his throat tightened in anguish. *I hope she's holding her breath.*

Above the motor's roar, he sensed more than heard something from the shore. He risked glancing toward the crowd. They were pointing to Josh's left, their mouths moving, but their words unheard.

Josh twisted his head in the direction of the pointing, but he saw nothing. He eased off on the throttle and circled, silently praying that he would not kill the engine.

He saw her then. Her head was back and her arms were flung out to the side in the violent waters. *She's dead!* The thought hit him like a sledgehammer as he steered toward her. *No! Maybe she's trying to float and save her strength!*

He glanced back to see Tank freeing his right hand while holding on to the inner tube's rope with the other. Suddenly, the motor coughed and the jet ski slowed.

"Oh, no!" Josh cried aloud, glancing down but automatically swerving away so he wouldn't run into the helpless girl.

The motor caught and ran smoothly again. *Thanks, Lord!* Immediately, Josh tried to relocate Alicia. He had passed her, so he turned as sharply as he dared and headed back toward her.

She raised her head and weakly lifted one arm above

the deadly white water.

"Hang on!" Josh shouted, doubting she could hear him. "We're going to . . . uh-oh!"

He felt an incoming wave lift the jet ski and slide past him. It seized the girl and carried her rapidly toward the yawning cavern.

Can't let her go back in there again! Josh told himself, advancing the throttle. *She might not be strong enough to survive.* Then he also realized something else. *If the wave carries this jet ski into there . . .*

He turned to glance over his shoulder. Even through the spray hitting Tank, Josh could see that his friend's face was pale and drawn. *Scared to death,* Josh realized. *Well, so am I! We're going to get only one chance!*

He opened the throttle wide and sped past Alicia, who now was dangerously close to the cave. He changed the jet ski's direction so that the momentum swung the trailing inner tube close to her.

It's up to you, Tank! Don't miss!

Josh saw his friend's right arm stretch out and Alicia's hand weakly reaching for it.

"Grab her, Tank!" Josh shouted. "Grab . . . . Yes!"

With a mighty heave, Tank clutched Alicia's wrist and pulled. She slid toward him and onto the inner tube.

Josh didn't wait to see any more. He turned around just in time to keep from running full speed into the basin's rocky sides.

"Ohhhhh!" he yelled, changing direction at the last

moment. Then he roared out of the wild water toward the narrow channel. He risked a glance back. Tank and Alicia bounced along on the inner tube. Tank seemed to be grinning, but the way the spray hit him in the face, Josh couldn't be sure.

He heard wild cheering from the watching crowd. He let out a joyful and triumphant yell and headed the jet ski and its trailing inner-tube cargo toward safety.

Chapter Thirteen

AN ALASKAN SURPRISE

That night, Alicia's father rented a large room at a Waikiki Beach* hotel for what had suddenly become a combination going-away party and celebration of life.

Everyone knew that Alicia, along with Josh and Tank, could have been killed. Instead, there was jubilation that they were alive and well. This good feeling caused old animosities to be forgotten.

Josh stood apart, listening to the stereo music. He was happy but also a little sad because Tank and his family were moving to Alaska. Josh looked around for his best friend but didn't see him. Instead, Josh's gaze touched his and Tank's parents at the front door. Alicia and her father had just arrived and were talking to the other adults.

Josh's eyes moved across the room, over the other adult neighbors and young people who were present. Josh's and Tank's sisters were chatting with Manuel.

Beyond them, Josh stared at Roger, who was talking with King Kong. The neighborhood bully had never been invited to a party before. But Josh learned that late that afternoon, Alicia had personally gone to Kong's house and asked him to come.

I never expected him to accept, Josh thought. *Well, I guess even Kong can change.*

Kong had even dressed like the other boys, in a clean aloha shirt and long pants. His usually tousled hair was neatly combed, and there was no sign of his infamous black leather gloves.

Even so, Josh noticed that the other kids were suspicious and kept their distance from the bully. But with Roger breaking the ice, Josh believed that soon they also would be speaking to Kong.

I'd better do that right now, Josh told himself. He started across the room, stopping briefly to talk to other kids from his neighborhood, school, and church. They turned to follow him with their eyes as he approached Kong.

Tank left some friends and called, "Hey, Josh, wait up!"

Josh nodded and stopped as Tank worked his way through the crowd.

"Some party, huh?" Tank commented.

"Best I've ever seen," he admitted, studying his friend's face. Except for a slightly turned-down mouth, Tank was hiding the pain of his having to move to Alaska.

"Well, at least we had one last exciting adventure together," Tank commented. "We helped capture the poachers and then rescue Alicia. Personally, I've had enough adventures for a while."

"Me, too. Only I still sort of wish we could have some Alaskan experiences together." Josh sighed and shook his head. "But some things just don't seem to work out."

Alicia walked up. "I'm glad I caught you two together," she said softly.

"Are you all right now?" Josh asked.

"Yes. I slept all afternoon. I'll be fine now," she replied. "I just want to say again how much I appreciate you and Tank saving my life this afternoon and for saying you forgive me."

It hadn't been easy to forgive, but Josh had finally genuinely done that. "We all make mistakes," he said. "And we all need forgiveness."

"Thank you, Josh. I want to be sure you and Tank understand why I did those foolish things." Without waiting for their response, she continued. "Before I came here, I had heard about the adventures you two had. I wanted to prove to both of you that I could do the same or more, even though I'm a girl. So I did some dumb things. But I learned my lesson in the Witch's Cauldron. Believe me, I'm a changed girl."

Josh nodded approval. "Showing off and doing dangerous things isn't the way to make people like you. But I was impressed when you showed concern for Roger when Kong tried to bully him a few days ago. And inviting Kong was a very special thing to do."

"Yeah," Tank agreed, glancing across the room where Roger and Kong were actually laughing together. "I'm impressed, too. Alicia, I feel better about maybe having you as a neighbor in Alaska."

She smiled warmly. "I'm glad you mentioned that. It reminded me of something I've got to do." She turned and motioned toward the adults standing by the front door. They nodded and headed toward the microphone. Alicia took each of the boys by their hands, saying, "Come with me."

"What's going on?" Josh asked as they were led through the crowd, which parted to let them pass.

"You'll see," Alicia replied mysteriously.

Josh went reluctantly. *We're going to be embarrassed in front of all these people*, he told himself. *Why do adults have to make such a big deal out of things like this afternoon?*

Josh glanced at Tank and guessed that he was thinking the same thing. Josh saw that Tank was quietly trying to escape Alicia's grip. Josh also tried, but it was useless. They followed Alicia to where all five adults waited by the upright microphone.

Mr. Wharton spoke into it, his voice booming across the room. "May I please have everyone's attention?" As the crowd quieted and faced him, he asked that the music be turned down for a minute. He motioned to his daughter. "Alicia, have the boys stand here beside me, please."

She obeyed, then stepped back with the other adults.

Josh glanced at his parents, then Tank's. All four seemed to be suppressing smiles. Josh squirmed, feeling even more embarrassment at all the fuss.

Mr. Wharton's voice echoed from the speakers. "I can

see by the agonized looks on Josh's and Tank's faces that they don't want any more said about the heroic actions they performed this afternoon. My daughter and I will be forever grateful for those boys' courage, as we have told them many times in the last few hours. So we'll spare the boys and talk about something else."

Josh was so surprised, he automatically turned to Tank, who shrugged, showing he had no idea what was going on.

Alicia's father continued addressing the crowd. "As you know, my daughter and I are returning to Alaska. You also know that Mr. Catlett has decided to accept his company's promotion to an Alaskan store. I'm sure you'll all miss them."

Applause greeted this comment, but Josh didn't join in. He still couldn't figure out what was happening.

"What you don't know," Mr. Wharton said, "is that I became fascinated with what Mr. Ladd does with his tourist publication. So I made him an offer that I didn't think he could refuse."

Josh's heart plummeted. In sudden anguish, he whispered to Tank, "Oh, no! He's going to buy out Dad's paper!"

Tank groaned and rolled his eyes upward.

Alicia's father turned to Mr. Ladd. "John, will you step up here and tell these nice people what your decision is?"

Josh prayed silently, *Dear Lord, please don't let him sell out!*

Mr. Ladd moved to the mike. "Trent Wharton has offered to buy a half-interest in my Hawaii publication and provide the capital needed to expand our operation."

Josh glanced at Tank, who stared in surprise.

"There is a condition," Mr. Ladd continued. "In exchange, I'm to start a similar tourist publication in Alaska."

"What?" Josh and Tank cried together.

Mr. Ladd grinned at his oldest son. "Josh, I've already talked with your sister and little brother. If you agree with them, your mother, and me, the Ladd family will move to Alaska and be neighbors with Tank's and Alicia's families. What do you say?"

Josh's eyes opened wide. He gulped but could not answer.

His father chuckled. "From the look on your face, son, I think I'd better explain a little more." He turned to again face the crowd. "That means we'll have businesses here in Hawaii and in Alaska. So we'll have to travel back and forth between the two states from time to time. So, Josh," his father concluded, "what's your decision?"

The boy's face lit up. He thumped Tank on the back and yelled, "I say yes!"

The crowd broke out in cheers as Josh and his best friend hugged each other and whooped with joy.

"We're going to be together after all!" Josh shouted in Tank's ear. "And we're going to have a whole bunch of new adventures in Alaska's wilderness!"

"Yeah!" Tank joyfully shouted. "I can hardly wait for the first one! Look out, Alaska! Here we come!"

GLOSSARY

CHAPTER 1

Scuba (SKOO-ba): Stands for "self-contained underwater breathing apparatus." It's a way of diving with a portable breathing unit consisting of compressed air in tanks, hoses, and a mouthpiece. This gear allows free-swimming divers to go deeper than almost anyone had dreamed possible a few years ago.

Kapali (kah-PAH-lee): Hawaiian for "the cliff." The Anglo-Saxon word "Clive" also means "cliff."

Wahine (wah-HEE-nee): Hawaiian for "female."

Haole (HOW-lee): A Hawaiian word originally meaning "stranger," but now used to mean "Caucasian" or "white person."

Sugarcane: Hawaii is famous for its many plantations where very tall stalks of cane are grown. After harvesting the cane, sugar is extracted for use around the world.

Waikiki (WHY-kee-kee): The area or district of Honolulu around the famous beach. Waikiki is Hawaiian for "spouting water."

Honolulu (hoe-no-LOO-LOO): Hawaii's capital and the most populous city in the fiftieth state; located on the island of Oahu. In Hawaiian, Honolulu means "sheltered bay."

Local: A term used in Hawaii for a brown- or yellow-skinned person who lives in the area but is not necessarily native born.

CHAPTER 2

Ironwood tree: A leafless tree with long, drooping green needles. Sometimes called an Australian pine, in Hawaii this tree is used as a windbreak.

Kauai (kuh-WYE): A Hawaiian island northwest of Oahu (where Honolulu is located). Kauai is thought by many to be the most photogenic of the islands.

Lihue (lee-HOO-ee): A principal city on Kauai's southeast side.

CHAPTER 3

Diamond Head: The 760-foot-high extinct volcano at the east end of Honolulu. It's the most prominent Honolulu volcanic landmark.

Oahu (oh-WAH-hoo): Hawaii's most populous island and the site of its capital city, Honolulu.

Lanai (LAH-nye): Hawaiian for "patio," "porch," or

"balcony." Also, when capitalized, Lanai is a smaller Hawaiian island.

Cul-de-sac (KUL-da-sak): A street closed at one end. It's from the French words meaning "bottom of the sack."

Oleander (OH-lee-an-der): A poisonous evergreen shrub with white, pink, or red flowers.

Be-still tree: A short, poisonous tree with dense green foliage and bright yellow flowers that fold up at night.

Buddhist (BOO-dist): A person who follows the religion that grew out of the teaching of Guatama Buddha.

Board-and-batten: A house with a particular style of siding. Wide boards or sheets of lumber are set vertically, and the joints are covered by small strips of wood (battens).

Akamai (AH-kah-my): Hawaiian for "smart."

Maui (MAU-ee): Second largest of the main Hawaiian islands. It is 728 square miles in area.

Kamuela (kah-muh-way-LAH): Hawaiian for "Samuel."

Bruddah (BRUD-duh): Pidgin English for "brother."

Pidgin English (PIDJ-uhn): A simplified version of English. It was originally used in the Orient for communication between people who spoke different languages.

Da kine (dah kine): Pidgin English for "the kind." This is an expression and not usually translated literally.

Pupule (poo-POO-lay): Hawaiian for "crazy."

CHAPTER 4

Plumeria (ploo-MARE-ee-ah): Also called frangipani
(FRAN-gee-PAN-ee). A shrub or small tree that pro-
duces large, very fragrant blossoms. They are popu-
lar in leis.

CHAPTER 5

Papaya (pa-PIE-yah): A large, oblong, yellow fruit common in Hawaii.

Guava (GWAW-vah): A sweet, yellow fruit growing wild
in tropical areas and common in Hawaii.

Vietnam War (VEE-et nahm): A war in an Asian country
where U.S. military forces suffered their only
defeat in history. Americans were deeply divided
over involvement in this war, which ended
in 1973.

Aloha shirt (ah-LOW-hah): A loose-fitting man's Hawaiian
shirt worn outside the pants. The garment is usually
very colorful.

CHAPTER 6

Perks: Short for "perquisites" (PER-kwah-zets), which are
benefits, profits, or privileges given in addition to a
regular salary or wages.

Lahaina (lah-HIGH-nah): A seaport town of 6,100 on the
northwest coast of Maui. Once the whaling capital of
the mid-Pacific, it's now a center of tourism, shop-
ping, and pineapple and sugarcane farming.

Kiawe (key-AH-vay): A very thorny algaroba or mesquite tree that grows mostly in dry areas. Kiawe may reach sixty feet in height.

Muumuu (MOO-oo-MOO-oo): A loose, colorful dress or gown frequently worn by women in Hawaii. This word is sometimes mispronounced as "moo-moo."

CHAPTER 7

Flukes (floo-ks): Lobes on a whale's tail; the flat part of a whale's tail; either half of the triangular tail of a whale.

Makaha (mah-KAH-ha): An entrance or exit from an enclosure.

Lava tube: A hollow tube made when hot lava flowed across the land. The outside lava hardened first, forming a crust through which the hot interior lava continued to flow. Eventually, most of the lava drained out of the inside, leaving a tunnel or tube.

CHAPTER 8

Whan: Hawaiian for "one."

Planty (PLANT-ee): Pidgin English for "plenty."

Naupaka (nah-oo-pah-KAH): A native Hawaiian shrub growing near the coast. It has white or light-colored blossoms that look like half flowers.

CHAPTER 10

Punchbowl: This 498-foot-tall hill, an extinct volcano at Honolulu, is the site of the National Cemetery of the

Pacific. Thousands of World War II dead are buried here.

Pearl Harbor: This American naval base in Hawaii was the target of a surprise attack by Japanese naval planes early on the morning of December 7, 1941. There was a heavy loss of life when 188 planes were destroyed. More than twenty ships were sunk or heavily damaged. This resulted in the United States declaring war against Japan, eventually forcing unconditional surrender.

Arizona: The American battleship *Arizona* was sunk at Pearl Harbor in the Japanese surprise attack on Sunday morning, December 7, 1941. The ship took a direct bomb hit and sank in nine minutes with a loss of 1,177 lives. The bodies were never recovered. A glistening white memorial now spans the sunken vessel.

CHAPTER 11
Heah: Pidgin English for "here."
Malihini (mah-lah-HEE-nee): Hawaiian for "newcomer."
Mahalo (mah-HA-lo): Hawaiian for "thanks."

CHAPTER 13
Waikiki Beach (WHY-kee-kee): Hawaii's most famous white sand beach.

The Dangerous Canoe Race (#4)
Josh and his friends paddle into peril by racing a bully willing to do anything to win.

Mystery of the Island Jungle (#3)
Josh must find the courage to free his friend from a vicious stranger.

The Legend of Fire (#2)
Josh attempts to rescue his father from kidnappers and an erupting volcano.

Secret of the Shark Pit (#1)
The Ladds brave a life-or-death race for hidden treasure.

$4.99 each

Available at your favorite Christian bookstore.

Breakaway

With colorful graphics, hot topics and humor, this magazine for teen guys helps them keep their faith on course and gives the latest info on sports, music, celebrities . . . even girls. Best of all, this publication shows teens how they can put their Christian faith into practice and resist peer pressure.

All magazines are published monthly except where otherwise noted. For more information regarding these and other resources, please call Focus on the Family at (719) 531-5181, or write to us at Focus on the Family, Colorado Springs, CO 80995.